Leap

Diamondsong

A Concerto in Ten Parts

Part 08:
Leap

E.D.E. Bell

Atthis Arts
Detroit, Michigan

Diamondsong

Part 08: Leap

This is a work of fiction.
Any resemblance to actual pyrsi, winged or otherwise, is purely coincidental.

Cover Art by M.C. Krauss

Map of Ada-ji by Ulla Thynell

Interior Design by G.C. Bell

Editorial Services by:
Catherine Jones Payne, Quill Pen Editorial
Kelsey Ronan
M. Cusack

Published by Atthis Arts, LLC
Detroit, Michigan
atthisarts.com

ISBN 978-1-945009-58-7

Library of Congress Control Number: 2020933203

First Edition: Published April 2020

This book is dedicated to Tad Williams.

I hope I can give to others
any measure of what you've given me.

Preface

Unlike the rest, the title for this volume wasn't selected until after it had been written. I didn't think the original title fit, and I couldn't land on a new one. The story jumps between themes: it's a little art, a little soul, a little spark, and then amidst all that, its imagery turned out much more direct than I'd originally envisioned. After all my self-doubt and worries about how to speak and not to speak, I pushed forward with this one—with Dime better articulating what she has been discovering all along. That so much boils down to power—and that pyrsi who try and take power, specifically disproportionate power, must not be excused. This isn't politics. It's our charge.

I landed on *Leap*.

I really hope you enjoy it. I owe much to the team, who are the ones throwing water at me as I see that finish line in the distance. The ones telling me this serial matters, and we're gonna do it together. Thanks to Catherine Jones Payne for careful and insightful developmental edits, Kelsey Ronan for great advice on the line, and to my team of friends: Meghan Cusack, Camille Gooderham Campbell, Sasha Kasoff Moore, Laura Johnson, Deborah Reilly, and Maria Judge.

I was so positive about the advent of spring this year, but then it turned out much harder than I could have imagined—for all of us. Yet it's still spring, and the joy of warmth and growth is bursting around me. We struggle through it, but I remain so positive about our future. We just can't give up on it.

Thanks for reading my story.

E.D.E. Bell

April 2020

The World of Ada-ji

The Ja-lal: A humanoid species, dwelling in the foothills and plains of Ada-ji, characterized by broad advancements in construction, invention, and health. The Fo-ror call them brutes.

The Fo-ror: A winged humanoid species, dwelling in the forests of Ada-ji, characterized by their natural living and the use of magical powers, known as valence. The Ja-lal call them fairies.

The Ja-lal and Fo-ror are similar in form, with gray skin, but differences between them in composition and culture. Pyr is singular for a Ja-lal or Fo-ror and pyrsi is plural.

The pyrsi of Ada-ji hold many **gender identities**. While this doesn't clarify all aspects of gender, it is polite to introduce oneself with a prefix, indicating the appropriate pronouns:

- **Fe'** indicates a set of feminine identities, using the pronouns she/her/her(s).
- **Ma'** indicates a set of masculine identities, using the pronouns he/him/his.
- **Ji'** indicates a set of spectrum identities, using the pronouns ve/ver/vis.

When gender is unknown, it is polite to refer to a pyr with xe/xem/xyr(s). Any group of pyrsi (plural) would be referred to with they/them/their(s).

A pyr may be generically referred to as **Burge**, short for the more formal Burgess, often for purposes of polite address or getting a stranger's attention. This is similar to the use of Sir or Ma'am on Earth. For those who hold social prejudice based on class, the term implies some sense of status or honor.

Ja-lal and Fo-ror may live up to 50 cycles. Their lives are divided into defined **epochs**, aligning with societal expectations:

Aoch Age 0-9 — Characterized by upbringing, education, and exploration

Bakh Age 10-19 — Centered on building family, performing and completing apprenticeships, and finalizing life plans

Gamh Age 20-29 — Fully immersed in their specialty or role, contributing full-time to society

Dorh Age 30-39 — Respected in leadership and/or advisory roles; it is normal to take some time for self

Eroh Age 40+ — Expected to retire and engage in craft or occasional consulting, through the **life expectancy of around 50 cycles**.

Expectations differ for each culture. For example, while a Ja-lal must develop xyr profession into a career, a Fo-ror's profession and rank are set based on xyr social class and other historical and cultural factors.

A **cycle** on Ada-ji is perhaps up to four times the length of an Earth year. So, our main character, at age 20.5 cycles, has lived more than 80 Earth years but, in relation to her life span, could be considered at the **maturity of her early forties** on Earth.

Each **turn** on Ada-ji, a period of day and then night, is **significantly longer than an Earth day**. As such, pyrsi do not sleep according to light or dark, but instead based on their own needs, lifestyle, profession, and schedule.

The Ja-lal measure time by the periodic sounding of bells; they refer to the resultant time periods with the same term. The Fo-ror are less rigid about time-keeping and refer to the equivalent time period as a span. Each **bell**, or **span**, consists of more than two Earth hours.

Smaller amounts of time are referred to by both cultures as **takes**, which can be thought of as about ten Earth minutes.

In Earth terms, it has been about seven weeks since the beginning of our tale.

The Ja-lal and Fo-ror live on separate sides of the Great Cliff. They have not interacted since the *Great War*, an event most noted for being the **end of the Violence** on Ada-ji.

Synopsis to Here

Just after Dime had left her career working for the Circles, the government of the Ja-lal, three hooded figures burst into her home, determined to take her away. Dime and her spouse, Dayn, ran to escape them.

The intruders were revealed to be Fo-ror, commonly called fairies. These fairies, unseen since the conclusion of the Great War, were feared and loathed by the Ja-lal, who were taught that any contact would cause the Violence to return.

Dime escaped the city and was rescued by a large animal species known as newts, where she befriended a young newt she called Juni. Dime was found there by a fe'pyr familiar with fairies, Ella, who broke the news that Dime was biologically a Fo-ror—one whose wings had been removed.

Later, Ella explained that the magical fairy power of valence did not come from the wings, but from the heart. At her recommendation, Dime traveled to the diamond caves, where she confirmed and practiced her powers. There, she discovered that the Ja-lal also have powers of valence, more internally directed. Dime believes very few Ja-lal are aware of, and thus intentionally shaping, their own powers.

Trying to make sense of these events, Dime traveled between the lands of the fairies, the Heartland, and her own Sol's Reach. She reconnected with friends: Zael, who is dying, Ador, the founder of an advocacy group called the Free Winds, Ador's spouse Batu, and Dime's own family: Dayn, Luja, and Tum. She was surprised to run into Rock, an Intel Agent and former flame, with whom she has developed a complicated friendship.

She encountered new allies: Volana, a fairy connected to a secret Fo-ror discussion group, the Foundry, Volana's friend Uchitar, who struggles with tzetz-addiction, and Hin, a young assistant Ador has taken under his charge.

While in the Heartland, Dime was approached by an officer of a political group, the Risers, named Intinpalo. He believes in the superiority of the Fo-ror, but an encounter with Dime's father, Gorg, may have left an impression.

Dime met with the leaders of each land. First, High Seat Ferala, who confessed that Dime was part of an old scheme to avenge the horrors of a disease called the curse, which the Fo-ror blamed on the Ja-lal. This scheme, designed by now Third Seat Neimano, was named Project Diamondsong. His plan was to remove the wings from Fo-ror newborns, place them in positions of potential influence amongst the Ja-lal, and then allow them to grow up before activating their loyalties as Fo-ror spies. Later, she met with Sala, the Light, who was resistant to her message of working with the Fo-ror.

Dime has been able to locate four other victims of Neimano: Kolk, Nafat, Olok, and now Jaza, the leader of the Sol's Pillars herself.

Additionally, Dime has learned that the newts hold emotion-based valence. Stern Eyes used hers to shock Neimano, causing him to fly away, clearly injured, after he tried to attack Dime once again.

Feeling the urgency of bringing more voices to their cause, Dime and her family traveled to a place known as the Underground, where Fo-ror and Ja-lal live together in secret.

Dime returned alone to Lodon, preparing to take action. Soon after, she learned that her children had flown back to the newts by fairy transport, Uchitar was being held in Fo-ror prison, and Rock was perhaps being held by the Sol's Pillars. She revealed her history to Hin, who asked to be left alone. Ador is concerned and disappointed regarding Hin's continued reservations toward working with the fairies.

Volana and Dime traveled to the prison and removed Uchitar from custody, with Seat Layanie assisting their departure after a tense encounter with Neimano in the corridors. Back by herself in Lodon, Dime found that Jaza was pyrsonally holding Rock captive. Dime helped Rock get away, and then returned, tired, to Sala's office, where she made an additional plea for her cooperation.

Dime, still in Lodon, sees the paths to peaceful change crumbling in every direction. She has decided that learning more about Neimano's other victims is her best next step.

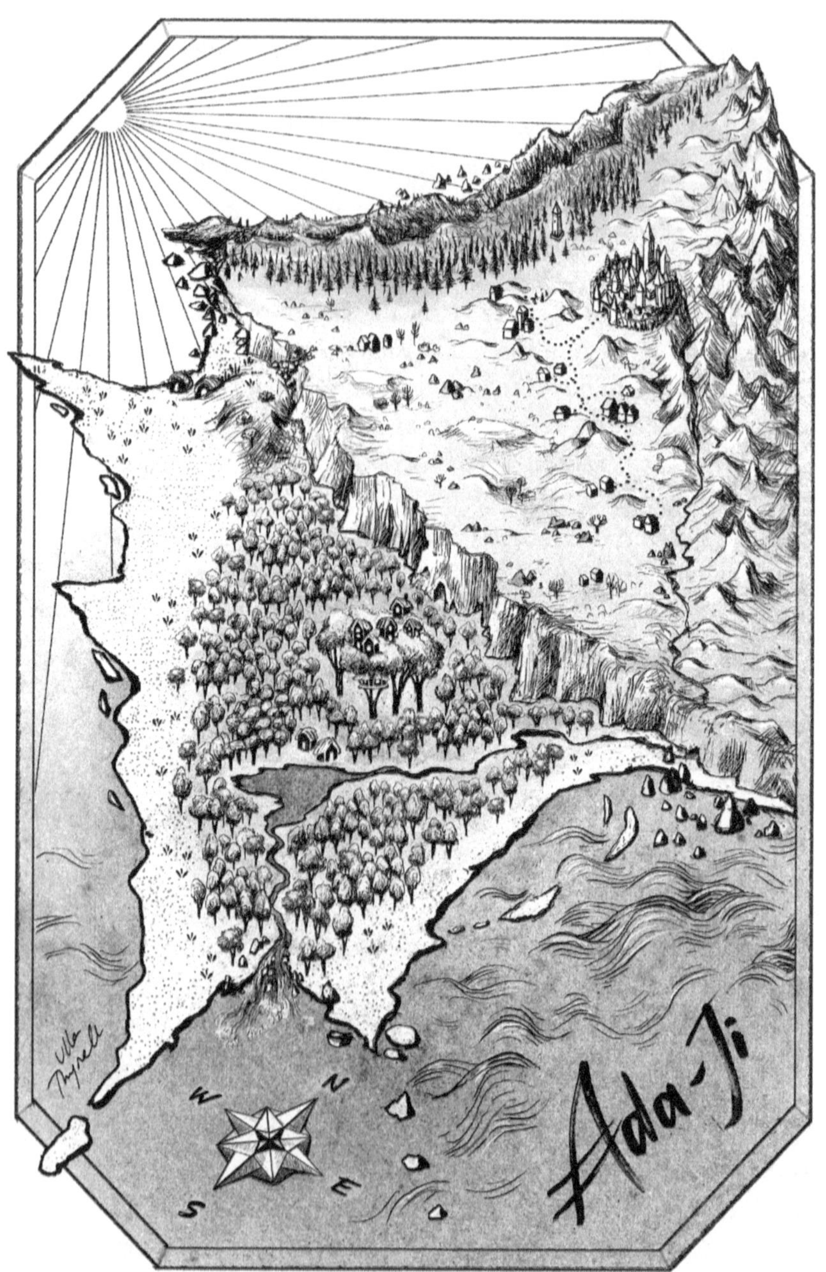

Ada-Ji
N
S
E
W

Leap

Had I known how close we were to war,
I would have certainly spoken out.

—Aletta Jacobs, *Memories*, 1924, reflecting on 1912

Act 1

PATHWAYS

Great Sol, Batu's home had a nice shower. The private, enclosed space streamed luxuriously warm water, with no alarming bursts of hot or cold. A carved dome of soap gave off a scent in the steam that let her imagine she was lounging inside of a whitepetal garden. Even the tile patterns on the walls posed like works of art, a mix of deep blues and soft greens in a blend of geometry and flow; Dime could have stared at them indefinitely.

But she could not relax. Not truly. Despite the here and there where she'd taken in the moment or forced a deep breath, she hadn't really relaxed since the turn she left her career. Though she didn't burden the others with it, that worried her a lot. Sure, the return of the Great War worried her more. But one worry did not preclude another. The point was, she'd been telling herself all along that when this was over, she'd be able to relax again. *This.* Always *this.*

What was *this*? And when was *that*? She stretched back, coaxing the ache in her shoulders. There was no endpoint in sight. No declaration that things were fine; harm was over. So, then, when could she take some time and simply exist? Pyrsi needed rest—it was like food, or water.

If there was that time, it wasn't this turn.

She stepped out and got dressed, patting her black velour suit as something at least familiar. Though she didn't really need the device yet, pyrsi at the Underground had shown her how to run a little toothed handtool through the hair on top of her head. This "brush" felt nice, actually, and she ran it through a few more times, enjoying the massage against her scalp. She wondered if this was damaging her tattoos. It shouldn't.

A knock sounded at the door.

"Come in," Dime said, not turning to see Rock walk into the room. The door clicked shut.

"I want to go with you."

Dime set down the brush. It wasn't as though she hadn't thought of it. Having Rock nearby made her feel more secure. But Rock stuck out in fairy lands, and that's where Dime would end up going.

Yet, Dime stuck out too.

"Stop rehashing it. I want to go, and I think you know it's a good idea." Rock was staring at the carved owl on the bedside table. She hadn't mentioned it, but Dime could tell she'd been thrilled to see that the bulky statue hadn't been discarded in all of Dime's travels.

"Hoo!" Dime whispered.

Rock glared at her.

"Ok, fine. I was on the wall over it and if you're so interested, that will break the tie. I want to leave soon, though. Like, pretty much now."

"D. Did I just break a tie between you and . . . yourself? Never mind. I'm ready to go when you are. And look, I'm not trying to glom on. If you need privacy for something, or whatever, just tell me."

"No, I know." She smiled at her friend. "Hey, I'm glad you'll be there. Takes a little weight off."

Rock's lip twisted, her blue lipstick taking on an almost purple sheen in the lamplight. Dime hadn't really thought before how the bright color distracted from her face. She tried to defocus on it. Rock's graying skin and rounded ridges came into view. She forgot, sometimes, how much older they both were.

"You're staring at me."

"Was picturing you without the lipstick. I like it, but you know."

"It's my signature look, D. Back off."

Dime made no effort to hide the rolling of her eyes, but they were both chuckling as they walked back into Batu's living space.

Batu wore her yellow drape—Dime still had no idea what to call it—again, though now over a mint green shirt and loose, peach-colored pants. She held out two cloth mealbags, which Dime stared at in fond disbelief before putting one of them in her backpack.

She'd considered stopping by to seek resolution with Hin, but Batu said he'd left to go work at one of the domes. "We talked," was all she'd wanted to say. "He needs some time," she'd added, though she didn't look thrilled and had quickly changed the subject.

Dime wasn't feeling like time was something they all had.

As they walked out into the stairwell, the city lights twinkling in the long windows, Dime glanced back up at the doorway. She caught just a blink of Batu's wistful gaze before it spread into a wide grin. "Pleasant travels!" Batu fanned her fingers. Dime did as well.

"We'll see you soon!" Rock said, and together they walked down the stairs.

No one really gets used to the reactions when pyrsi can't just let a pyr walk in peace, but Dime did her best to ignore the flutter of activity as she moved through the first tower hub. She avoided eye contact with two pyrsi about her own age who were clearly whispering about her while others gawked. As she turned, she caught eyes with a younger pyr whose stare seemed curious. "Hello," she said. The pyr glanced away.

Batu had urged Dime to walk openly through their tower and had insisted she not conceal where she was staying. "I'm tired of the rest of it," she'd said. "You be yourself. However you're comfortable."

Dime would never forget what that had meant to her. Even if the execution wasn't so easy. A pyr started and turned toward the brick wall, as if xe'd accidentally opened an occupied washroom door.

"Holy Sol," Rock muttered. "Get over it. Or sell merch. You

know, stare at Dazzling Diamond all day with this illustrated coaster set."

To that, Dime had to laugh. No one was going to put her on a coaster. Besides, it was night.

The strange reactions continued as they walked on in the direction of Nafat's new fairy-themed club. Batu's tower was upcity, and the location she'd given them was midcity, near the art district. The trip took close to a bell on foot, but they'd decided to walk anyway, as soon they'd be flying to the sur. Rock kept making conversation with her about buildings and shops that they passed, probably to distract from all the gapes and pointing fingers, but still, it felt like much longer. Dime was ready for about anything by the time they made their last turn.

While Nafat seemed to honor keeping his history secret for now, the fact that he'd named his group the Fairy Fanatics certainly conveyed his openness about fairy culture. So Dime wasn't worried about being seen with the ma'pyr; his club seemed a natural place for her to go. Yet, she had no idea what they were going to find there.

"So what are we doing?" Rock asked. "Suggesting he dial it back?"

"I don't know," Dime admitted. "Maybe? I just need to find out what Neimano's endgame is, and Nafat could be part of it, so I thought I'd swing by before we leave the city." She rubbed her hair. "Everyone expects me to have a definable reason for everything. Don't you ever just go places to see what you're missing?"

"Lead on, Dime-No-Reason."

"You know what I mean. Now, it should be around this curve." Dime peered at the street signs, checking her notes.

The location, near the edge of the art district, turned out to be a sizable dome with a ground-level entrance. The structure of it looked old, but it had clearly just been repainted and repaired, not quite to look new, but with a tasteful eye for natural wear and structural resonance.

She loved older architecture like this. Some of the newer domes were constructed to be easier to maintain, but there was something about attended details, indulgent accents, and asymmetric nooks that stirred her soul.

While expense was a factor, she'd always thought architecture relied even more on love. She thought of the tree homes of Volana's lower-class neighborhood. A thousand little touches—like crawling vines over simple trellises or colorful segments of glass—made that neighborhood feel like somewhere special, and none of those residents had extra resources to spare.

In Nafat's case, expense had clearly not been a constraint. Restoring the plaster motifs and sculptures of the street-facing walls had taken skilled labor, and each protruding curve shone with gilded accents. Even to someone not looking for the details, the carefully placed gilding added a richness and glow that changed the whole feel of the structure when compared to the other buildings lining the street. She'd love to see it in the daylight.

Any question whether Nafat was on-shift was erased before they even entered. He met them on the entrance path, his striped suit trimmed with groupings of tiny chimes that jingled as he walked. "Hello!" he called out. It had been a long walk, Dime supposed. Someone could have run ahead and told him. Still.

"Hi, Nafat. Nice to see you again."

"Dime!"

"This pyr," Rock muttered through unmoving lips before walking forward to extend the bridge. "Hello, I'm Fe'Rock. Dime's friend. Fairy-curious."

Nafat reached for her arms, shaking them a little in his excitement. "Burgess Rock, Ma'Nafat. I am so excited to show you both what we've done!"

They walked in, and Dime realized she'd half been expecting some tacky display surrounding informal gathering tables, like the Free Winds running an ad agency. Pyrquins with wings glued on. Confetti or something. Who knew. Instead, the room was styled like an art gallery—the layout tasteful with the exception of the sparkling *Fairy Fanatics* sign in the entrance.

The rounded ceiling had been painted dark, and accented with soft silvery and goldish dots like the nightlight from the skystones. The tiled floor was mostly empty, with an uneven array of glass-covered stands, a few fine padded benches, and a ring of art around the room's rich green walls. Bright lamps illuminated each piece, reflecting against the glass panes, their flickering light distinctly Ja-lal. Dime realized with a jolt that Nafat did have the ability to light the room with glowstones. She wondered if he knew.

Pyrsi sat on the benches, not noticing Dime as they absorbed themselves in conversation about each piece. She walked around and tried to take it all in, as Rock perused the other side of the room. One large painting of the forest made her feel as though she were standing in it. The artist had worked in perspective, with the wide trunks narrowing to a spray of green above. Assembled in five panels, there was no question it had been painted at its setting; she could feel the direction the breeze was wafting through the trees. She longed a stride for the cool air, the soft musk. Not a stride—what did they call it. A flap?

Another painting, this one in pastels, showed a fairy in a tree-based home. It was all wrong. The narrow room featured doors, not curtains, and the walls were built with a geometric structure more indicative of a Lodon tower room than of the way Heartland wood frames wandered through the trees. The fairy's wings were exaggerated: brighter and larger than in real life, and with impractical rigidity, settling any issue that perhaps this depicted a different culture outside of what she was familiar with in Pito.

A pyr noticed her with some shock, but then politely nodded and looked away. Dime exhaled.

She moved inward, gazing at the stands, impressed by how clean and clear the glass covers were. One item, a painted stone, was labeled as a spiritual symbol of Sha. She had seen similar stones around Pito's ground gardens, sometimes painted. This one looked made by a ch'pyr, with bright colors and a swift hand. Another stand held a wood ladle, with a distinct Fo-ror style. A spoon! It was literally a spoon. It looked real, sure, but it was a spoon.

The more authentic items, she guessed, had been smuggled through the Crossing. She wondered if Nafat knew that, or even knew of the isolated trading town. As she turned to see his proud grin, her gut wrenched. There were things she couldn't say. She knew how he felt, having a beautiful and interesting culture stolen from him, and his pull to reclaim it. But Lodon was beautiful and interesting too, and the fact was, Nafat was in no position to represent this culture to others. How could she say any of this to him?

Unsure, she just stood there as Nafat drew near.

"Well? What do you think?"

"I . . . I hope there will be more connections soon," she stumbled. "So that you can involve . . . additional pyrsi, from different places in the Heartland. And 'Fanatics', well. Solies. The Ja-lal are called solies by open-minded fairies. Could you imagine . . . Soly Fanatics?"

She'd kind of wanted to tell him to shut it down. But the pyrsi. They were here. They were here with a gravity that differed from the energy of the Free Winds. It all felt complicated, and Dime wasn't an authority either. She resolved to get Volana's opinion. Seeing Nafat's face dim, she quickly added, "You are impacting minds. It's a start. But it must grow."

The part about growth seemed to reassure him. "Yes." He scrunched his mouth. "What would you call it? I thought Fanatics had a nice ring."

"It does. But, perhaps—Heartland Cultural Center?"

Nafat's eyes shifted. At first Dime thought he didn't like the name, but then she realized he was already somewhere else. "Would you join me for a moment? In private?" he asked. Dime glanced over at Rock who nodded as Nafat led Dime off toward the back. He motioned into an office area, that was rather plain by Nafat's standards. She was sure he had plans for it. An image flashed before her of purple walls and tin ceilings. That wouldn't be so bad, really. Maybe everyone's office space needed a Nafat.

He kept his voice low, even after closing the door behind them. "I always feel like pyrsi are listening to me. That probably sounds off. It's a thing I've had. My whole life, I guess." He remained standing, his fingers intertwined.

"It's ok," Dime said, not sure what else to say.

"A fairy came here."

"Was—"

"Wait. Oh, I'm sorry. I didn't mean to interrupt. But it wasn't just a fairy. The Intel Circle Chief." He chewed over the words *Intel Circle.*

"The IC Chief was with—"

"No, not together! I'm sorry; I keep interrupting. But I'm not being clear. Separately. Already, pyrsi view me differently. They mention that I might know fairies, hoping I'll say something. Then they discuss you, say, 'You know it could be true that she has fairy valence. Maybe she's a fairy.' Then they look at me. I don't know if it's to tell them about you or they suspect it of me. And I want to tell them, and then I don't know if I should.

"Then, one showed up. A winged one, I mean. I'm glad you warned me; xe came in all friendly, acting like I was obsessed with fairies and not just trying to help. Didn't even introduce xemself! Xe said that xe was looking for my partnership: that xe was working with the IC on a secret task for the Light's Council, to bring pyrsi together."

Dime sucked in a tight breath. "Nafat, he was lying. I know, lying is the Violence. That's what makes pyrsi so confused how to deal with Neimano. He . . . lies."

"I'm not sure."

How many times did she have to—

"I'm not sure it was Neimano. Assuming that's the fairy who did this. In fact, I'm sure it wasn't. I've spent my whole life around pyrsi who serve and pyrsi who are served, and this was the former."

Dime had never seen pyrsi in that light, but then she'd spent her life around all classes; the distinction wasn't important to her. So Nafat was visited by . . . a servant? A High Guard, then? But that's right—Neimano hadn't come for her either; he'd sent three guards. And what, Nafat got one? That hardly seemed equitable. Yet, there had been no arrest. No ropes, she presumed, for Nafat would have mentioned that. Maybe Neimano had learned how that went over here.

"More," Nafat continued, "it made no sense as truth. Think about it. Xe was contacting me on behalf of the Light's Circle. But, then, why wouldn't Light Sala contact me directly? She knows my family. She frequents the museum. She wouldn't send a fairy into Lodon to tell me what she could tell me herself. I was . . . scared."

Dime wanted to ask what he'd told the guard—after all, Nafat was still here—but it seemed such a direct question. She was glad when he answered it.

"I told xem to leave. I said I knew what was done, and this pyr had no flight path with me." He looked up, his mouth pulled tight. "I heard that's how they say it."

"And xe took that how?" Dime didn't believe xe'd just said 'fine' and left.

"Xe said, 'So be it,' and left."

Close enough. Dime started to say she should be going too, but then remembered what else Nafat had said. "But the IC *was* here, also. That was . . . after the fairy?"

Nafat nodded. "He said they had questions about my work, and suggested the Light's interest. And I remembered what I'd considered the last time, and I just began to feel very uncomfortable. I'd spent two epochs being politely ignored by government leaders, except when they wanted something from me, and now all the sudden I'm quite interesting and my time and my consent and my feelings do not seem to be among their concerns."

Dime knew how that felt.

"So I told him the same thing. Not the flight part, but I said in my most pleasant voice that Light Sala was welcome to visit. Then I walked back into view, where all the guests could see me. He left."

"Weren't you worried about an order? Or a hemsa?" She didn't mean to ask so rudely, but she was gaining a sense of the impact of what it would mean to the Circles if pyrsi simply ... stopped following their orders.

"I should have been! But my view has been changing." He ran his hand, covered in gold jewelry, over his finely-tattooed scalp. "I suppose it's all making me stubborn."

Dime glanced at the closed door, knowing Rock was out there waiting. "I'm glad you stood up for yourself. Nafat, I don't like saying this, but Rock and I will need to be going soon. Before we can see much of the collection. I mostly wanted to see if you were alright." She almost added *and if you had any ideas that might help*. Then she realized he'd moved her away, back into his office. Another visit.

"I'm not here to ask of anything from you," she said.

The pyr's face became more serious, and for a flash, she saw someone she could relate to. Someone ... who shared something with her.

"Thanks," he said. "It's been tough for me."

The truth was, she did want to ask if maybe he had ideas on why so many of the pyrsi like them had been harmed or had passed to memory. But he'd offered up his new info right at seeing her. Then, that was enough. Maybe if there were no answers in the Heartland, she'd come back, but here was Nafat, not unlike Olok, just wanting to live and contribute in their own ways.

Dime couldn't live her own life anymore. Not for now.

That was a choice she'd made. Not the moment she'd ran from her home, the High Guards in pursuit. No, it was made the moment she'd returned to the Heartland. The moment she'd fixed Ferala in the eyes and asked him that simple question: *Why?*

"I really like your hair," Nafat said. "I hope it's not rude to mention it. But I ... supposed pyrsi might be telling you otherwise, so I wanted my opinion on the ledger."

"Thanks! You know, it doesn't feel as weird as you'd think. You get used to it."

Nafat seemed to be considering this. He motioned back to a kitchen area, through a second, windowed, door. "Can I get you anything? Refreshment?"

She tried not to chuckle. There was no way he knew how to use any of that equipment. "I'm fine, but thank you. Unless you have something prepared? My friend would love that." In fairness, they both liked to eat. But Rock was outside so she could get blamed for this one.

"Oh, I do." He walked over to a crate full of decorated metal tins and handed one to Dime. "Keep that, please. Do you want to see the collection? I've put so much together in such a short time; I think it's a great start."

She must have made a face. Pyrsi were always reading into her faces.

"What?" Dismay clouded him. "Is there a problem with it?" Dime scrambled to answer.

"I don't know how to say this, but not all of the items are authentic. Many are, I think," she hastened to add. "Based on what I know, anyway." It was strange to remember, Nafat had grown up so ingrained in Lodon culture he'd probably never considered he could just travel to the Heartland himself.

Not that she knew how things would go moving forward. Would each culture allow the other in? Would they try to prevent a pyr's free passage? She felt melancholy at the thought, but could no longer deem it out of reach. "When you're able to do so—if we can—you'll want to get some pyrsi involved. You know, pyrsi who live there."

His face fell. "Is it all wrong? I'm a curator; I thought I had an eye for it."

"You're an art curator. You have an eye for art. It is definitely art." Maybe not some of the trinkets in the stands, but taste was highly subjective, so she would never suggest something was *not* art.

Realizing that wasn't the point she intended anyway, she

changed her approach. "Fairies are pyrsi, as you know, with similar attributes and similar flaws. Making them *more* isn't the counter to making them *lesser*. And the more they can tell us their own story, the more accurately that story will be told. The more authentic pyrsi's understanding will be." She stopped, again realizing that she was speaking to Nafat as a fellow Ja-lal. "I'm sorry. I know it's complicated. And I'm just figuring it out, too."

"Will they reject us?" He said it quickly.

Dime remembered the reactions she'd faced in the Heartland, less troubling, in truth, than those she'd found here at home. She chose her words. "We should be who we are." There were a million facets to that, and as many considerations. Any statement was bound to oversimplify something. "My plan is to be thoughtful as I can and hope others will be, too. But don't forget, even when it feels like starting over, we're not. I'm Dime. And you're Nafat."

"Thanks," Nafat said. "I'll think about that."

"Yeah," Dime said with a chuckle. "That's something about this whole ordeal. I've had to think a lot."

Nafat looked confused as to what the response to that should be. Instead he offered a polite smile and gestured toward the door.

Together, they walked back into the main room, where Rock was engaged in lively conversation with a seated couple. Her arms spread across the back of the bench and one leg was propped onto the other. The couple seemed fully immersed in whatever Rock was saying, and Dime smiled to herself. She turned back to Nafat. "Don't take me wrong; there are some wonderfully impressive things here." Subconsciously, she glanced over at the spoon.

"That one's real," he said, a grin twitching onto his face. "I've seen many fine utensils in my turns, too, but never one like this. Here, I'll show you."

Lifting the glass cover with a small cloth that he hadn't been holding a stride ago, he held out the ladle. "Hold it, if you would."

Dime set down the tin at her feet and picked up the spoon. Not sure what she was supposed to do with the curved utensil, she dipped it through the air as though she were serving some stew. The wooden spoon had a natural weight and balanced nicely in her hands. The curve of its handle held the flow of nature, not unlike an ocean wave. Or one of the forged metal embellishments of a Lodon lamppost. Harm it, it *was* artistic.

"I see," she said. "It's lovely." Dime handed it back to Nafat. "I just learned something. Thank you."

But Nafat's eyes had cut toward the main entrance, where a stream of pyrsi was filtering in. At least a dozen more now stood inside, murmuring. "Word of your presence has arrived," he said to Dime.

Rock was making her way toward the two of them.

Dime sighed as Nafat placed the ladle back under the glass, tilting it to an aesthetic angle before closing the case and slipping the cloth into a pocket.

"It does that," she said. "For now, I move along. It's been a theme."

"What do you want, Dime?"

A hot tub. "World peace. No threat of the Violence. Pyrsi are all as happy as their natural force of choice allows them to be."

Nafat raised an eyebrow.

"Fine. I want to have somewhere I can be myself and not have to keep escaping."

The curator quieted, watching the door. "Probably not right now."

"I know," Dime said, stooping to pick up the decorated tin. She wasn't going to leave what were probably rather fancy treats behind. "And thanks again for these." She tapped the tin. "Be well, friend. It's been really nice to see you again."

"It has," he replied, meeting her eyes. Nafat burst into a gregarious grin and he swept over to the doorway. "Welcome! Welcome! I am curator Ma'Nafat of the Heartland Cultural Center. We just received a new piece. Would you like to see it?"

Rock's slight smile showed gratitude for the diversion, but she didn't speak as they edged through the crowd and out onto the street, not giving time for those who saw them to figure out how to react.

"Well, that was not what I expected." Rock finally said. "Any other errands in the city?"

Dime stared up at the distant upcity towers, quiet.

"Your friend? We can go if you want."

She shook her head, still not looking at Rock. "We can't." She'd already made that decision once, by heading downcity. But leaving Lodon's walls altogether would close that door for a much longer time. With his health, maybe forever.

Seeing Zael again had been on her mind since returning. There was too much now. There's no way she'd go unnoticed, and she couldn't know the consequences. Besides, Yorm had been her friend, too, and though her reaction had hurt Dime, Dime wasn't interested in reprising that discomfort. For either of them. As the last visit had ended with some tiny acceptance from Yorm and a great effort from Zael, Dime had an inherent sense she should leave it there. She would not go.

Perhaps it wasn't closing a door. Perhaps it was walking through it.

Dime realized she was having this whole conversation with herself, and she offered an apologetic glance. Rock seemed to understand.

"This way, then." Rock motioned, and Dime followed behind. "I have a place with some supplies," Rock said, "if you don't mind one more stop. My bag, some tools. I have a few paynotes too. To travel I was thinking we could—"

"What's that?" Dime interrupted as they took a sharp left, seeing what looked like a parade rumbling across the lamplit street. As they hastened ahead, she peered at the passing pyrsi, trying to make out who they were.

Rock noticed it first. "Oh, she's not playing around. Look. Pillars."

Dime strained to make out the blazing insignias of the Sol's

Pillars adorning the sashes, bags, and jackets of the marchers. By instinct, she stepped back, but Rock placed a hand on her arm, knowing her implicit permission.

"Oh, no," Dime whispered. Moving closer, she called out. "What's going on?"

"It's her!" A pyr gasped and others jostled to get a view of her in the dark.

"Yes, it's me. What's going on?"

The pyrsi she'd asked seemed hesitant to answer, but a pyr who hadn't yet noticed the additional commotion shouted, xyr voice echoing between the surrounding buildings. "Everyone! Join our freedom rally! Light Jaza herself will be there."

Light Jaza!

Whether Jaza had encouraged this or the Pillars had taken it on themselves, Dime was alarmed at the speed of escalation. "We made her mad."

"Yep."

Dime watched in growing disgust as a line of yellow banners waved past. "Think we should go? Or would it make it worse?"

"It's already worse."

"Might be good to see what we're dealing with," she said. "But I still want to stick with the plan." She knew Rock understood that meant traveling to the Heartland. "If we can."

As they merged into the crowd, the bustle grew such that most pyrsi couldn't see the two former IC agents, one with fairy blood and the other without, as they walked along the street. It helped being shorter than everyone else, Dime thought with a snort. She heard a pyr shout behind her, but she didn't turn around.

Slowing near the entrance, the line led them into an outdoor theater that sloped toward a raised stone platform at the bottom. Dime remembered the last time she'd been here; the expertly designed theatre was a staple of the art district. She and Zael had gone to see a long-form sung drama, so long even Dayn and Yorm had found excuses not to go. Not that she could reminisce, as Jaza was already speaking, her mouth pressed to the extensive cone and pipe system used to announce the acts. The bellowing pyr wore a bright orange shirt, short in length so that her midriff was exposed. Tight, light green pants flared out at the bottom over huge white heels. Despite the massive crowd gathered—far more than the theatre was designed to hold—Jaza stood out, unmistakably, as the one with the voice.

Unlike the clamor in the streets, here everyone hushed, straining to hear each word. Only a few children cried out, confused.

"What would Lodon look like," Jaza asked, "with your view obscured by a flurry of purple wings?" Shouts erupted, then subsided. "Each stone in Lodon was placed by your sweat, your toil. Would they swarm in from their hive of squalid huts and usher you aside? Would they rise to land on each level, peering in through your windows to see what treasures await?" A murmur passed through the crowd, more intense now.

"Lodon is yours. Your toil. Your greatness. And no one—no one—can take that from you. No one can destroy what you have built."

As the crowd exploded with cheers and shouted replies, Dime reeled at the irony of these remarks. The pyrsi surrounding her were not the high class. They were, as Jaza had indicated, laborers, small merchants. What would be taken from them? As she'd continued to understand better over the last turns, the high class of Lodon controlled its wealth, its laws, its rules. Jaza herself had great wealth and influence, yet she stood here, convincing a crowd of downcity laborers that fairies would take something from them. And this was on top of the less ironic, but simply sheer meanness of her words. That the fairies were inferior; that they were a nuisance rather than a neighbor.

The brutality almost knocked her backward, and Rock glanced at her with concern. She shook her head, signaling to Rock not to worry, but she felt disoriented. As she'd mulled over for a while now and Hin had also pointed out, the fairies had never been a part of

Lodon discourse, just an occasional aside. Back when Sol's Pillars were lingering at the fringes, they'd been about maintaining Lodon's classes, at least as Dime had always read them. Maintaining the social structure that held some up and offered others a place to climb.

Now, she understood, both were true. Jaza used fear to upset the disadvantaged of Lodon into maintaining power for the advantaged of Lodon, while keeping in her back pocket a loathing for fairies that she could tap into once she chose to form her army. Or perhaps it had just worked out that way. No, some of it may have worked out that way, but the loathing had always been there. Hidden in whispers.

Neimano had forced the issue by sending his guards to get Dime, and Jaza had jumped right in. *Army.* Dime looked around, realizing she was surrounded by scores of screaming pyrsi, united in their excitement over keeping pyrsi outside of their walls, based only on their differences—their bodies and their rich, beautiful culture. She felt sick. Yet seeing the number gathered here, she knew no coalition her friends could build, whether it was four or ten or a hundred, could stop Jaza's army by order or even force, if it came to that. Jaza continued to shout.

"Pyrsi think we'll let them, don't they?" Howls of dismay.

"I won't let them!" Cheers.

"We won't let them!" Cheers.

"There are no limits—*no limits*—to what we must do to defend our freedom!"

Dime's eyes met Rock's. Trying not to draw attention, they picked their way back to the top of the theater. Someone shouted that Dime was there, to call Enforcement. Another called her an insect and told her to stay away. From her home. She blocked the words, not acknowledging any of xem. Together, Dime and Rock stayed quiet as they broke through the back line, and as Rock pointed past the circle drive toward a narrow alley, between two block buildings on the other side.

As they stepped onto the drive, she saw two Enforcement officers next to a small toothcar. Pacing, they looked as helpless as Dime felt.

The higher-ranking officer started, recognizing Dime as she approached. "I wouldn't provoke them," Dime warned. "She is inciting them that the Violence is justified; they might not hesitate to use it against you. Let us work it. We'll talk to the Light. Let them speak, for now, as long as they go home. There needs to be a solution, but the Violence tonight will not be it. We are working it. Ok?"

Dime was surprised when the pyr nearly saluted. She nodded, and they went on their way, as the officers began arguing behind them. Then, she stopped. Gesturing to Rock, she slipped behind the back wall of a public washroom, in between the drive and the top of the theatre, but out of sight of the officers. Rummaging in a pocket, she pulled out a notepad and pencil, and scribbled a hasty note.

> It's me. I was at your rally.
>
> Like I told you earlier, I won't speak of you. I want you to know that. And I won't speak to you again. Your actions disgust me. Perhaps they disgust you too.
>
> I want to pass along something someone recently told me. It's not your fault. I can't ask you not to be angry. I'm angry. But you can use your hurt to harm or to help.
>
> Anyway. If I can't convince you, back off. Just, go. Let me work it.
>
> Bye.

She did not sign the note.

Sealing it with her best cornerfold and scribbling something as close to a Circles' cipher as she was comfortable—the Circles would use wax but this would have to do—she climbed up onto the low stone wall surrounding the theatre. From there, she could barely see the platform far below.

With a thread of valence, the note bobbed as if it were caught in the wind. There really wasn't a wind, but she made a good show of it. As the note landed on the platform, Jaza swept it up and shoved it into a pocket, while not stopping her speech nor looking in Dime's direction.

Rock shivered. "Alright, let's go." They hurried across the drive and into the alley, scanning around the edge to make sure no one was headed their way. Not seeing anyone, they left.

They didn't talk for a while. Rock led them further downcity and eventually into a nondescript tower and up several floors. She opened her mouth, then shut it, and simply rapped at a door. "She's got some of my stuff," was all Rock said.

The fe'pyr answered, looking as though she'd been asleep. Dime glanced at the door and saw the privacy turner had been flipped.

The pyr did not introduce herself to Dime, nor did she say much as Rock walked in. Uncomfortable, Dime stayed in the hallway, registering that the pyr hadn't made note of her hair. She ran a hand through it.

A take later, Rock emerged, alone, with a large travel bag. "It's not as large as yours," she said, unprompted. "But yours is ridiculous." Dime noted her clothes were also new: a soft blue shirt and sleek pants that complemented her rounded, muscular shape with long, easy lines.

"I said one stop, but it's technically two, if you like my idea. Your friend inspired me."

"Huh?" Dime wasn't sure what Rock was talking about, but she'd already trudged ahead. Trusting her, she followed.

They walked down the tower stairs and out toward a crossroads market, and then back behind a line of compost bins. Fortunately, bins in the city needed to be sealed, so there wasn't any smell except for a bakery up the street. Rock asked Dime to wait. "Don't get in trouble. I'll be back in two takes." Not wanting to lean against the compost bin or sit in the dusty street, Dime loitered awkwardly, hoping she wouldn't be noticed.

When Rock returned, she waved Dime over to a side alley. "I had them drop it back here. A weird enough delivery spot but I tipped them, so they didn't argue."

Dime peered down the alley to see a rather elaborate dark wood bench, made for three pyrsi. As she drew closer, she saw that thick scarlet cushions were tied to the bottom and back. The bench's frame was intricately cut-out, featuring twirling rose vines in deep relief. As finely made as it was, even Dime knew it was strictly out of vogue. And had been for a while.

"Check it out. Padding. Plenty of space." She winked. "I take care of you, see?"

"You got that in the clearance room, Rock. In the back corner with things an Eoch would find old-fashioned."

"I'm aghast," Rock responded. "Do you not value my paynotes?" She paused. "Ugh. I didn't even mean that as a fairy reference. Everything has connotations now."

"And will continue to for a while, I suspect." Dime didn't have any paynotes left, and she'd spent the ones Ella gave her. They'd had some in an account to start her music school, but she didn't know if Dayn had accessed those by now. Dime sort of doubted she could just walk into a teller at this point, either way. "Both of our savings will be gone by the time this is done."

"Let's hope it's worth it," Rock said, grinning but with a tone of resignation.

Dime ran her hand over the cushions. "They feel new. Sort of. How long has this been in the shop? Anyway, you're distracting me. The point is, that 'rally' was horrific, and I feel like the obvious choice is to stay here and do something about it. But I'm not going to, unless you really disagree. I still want to chase my hunch and see if there's more to know about Neimano. I *feel* like there's more."

"I always vote hunch." Rock sat down on one side, swinging her legs, though artificially, since her feet hit the ground on each pass. "We can't work all of it. But you have a unique connection and might find a piece that we need. Let's go with that."

Dime leaned back, staring at the compost bins. "He started this. He put me here. He tried to take me. And *her*." Dime couldn't say Neimano *made* Jaza, but there was no question that without him, she would not be doing what she was. "So the question isn't as much what was he trying to do, but what is he trying to do now?

What danger is there to the rest of us? To everyone? I thought about something else, too.

"If something . . . if something bad happened to me, yeah, pyrsi care about me and it would be sad. But it's more than that. What if something happened to me, and that act started a War because suddenly more pyrsi cared? Because I became a symbol. More of a symbol. Whatever. Look, I'm happy protecting myself for the first reason, but there are other reasons too, is what I'm trying to say. We just don't know enough. There's more. There has to be more. And if we don't know it, then we might be shielding ourselves from each gust of wind when there's a whole tornado ready to hit. Anyway. I'm convinced. We can't lose sight of where this started. Not Jaza. Not Sala. Not the Free Winds. *Neimano*."

"I said I was fine with the hunch," Rock offered. "But feel free to continue." For once, Dime knew she was kidding. Rock loved facts and puzzles and was listening intently.

"So here's the next question. Do we walk on in and ask Ferala to tell me anything he hasn't? Appeal to his . . . goodness or sense of urgency? Why would he do it now if not before? But he has to be the one who knows— Wait, that's it."

Rock, her arms now draped across the arched frame, raised her eyebrows.

"No, listen. Who knows the most about the Seats? Not the Seats. The High Clerk."

"I take it this is someone you've met?"

"I have. It was the pyr at the gathering, at commons. The one who sat just offstage. He's really nice. Ma'Tikinal. He helped me get out of the complex after I almost got trapped in Ferala's office. Back when you gave me your key." And when she and Volana had encountered him in the Seats' complex, he'd seemed glad to see her. She hoped. "That's who we need to find. Here, let's talk about it on the way."

At first they set their bags between them on the bench, but then realizing that was actually more awkward, they moved them to the outsides.

"Ella had a good idea with the storage box," Rock conceded.

Sure, but Dime was still thinking about finding Tikinal. "Assuming there is no catastrophe in Pito—which, I know we can't assume given what we just left—the Seats traditionally reconvene at first bell, or whatever that's called in spans. Which means Tikinal is probably not there."

"Meeting once a turn still seems odd to me," Rock mused.

"I know, but it's convenient at the moment."

"True."

"So we just have to get Tikinal to work early."

"I have a feeling you can do that." Rock chuckled.

"Yeah, but I don't want to alert the Seats yet. Still, as jumpy as they are likely to be, getting Tikinal called in shouldn't take much. Oh, hey, one team question."

"Go."

"I trust Tikinal. I just really like him in some inherent way, and I don't have the energy to explain that in more normal words. I'd like to tell him the real situation. All of it. Will that be fine with you? I think that gives us the best chance of him being able to help."

Rock paused. "Yes. Tell him." She clapped her hands together, making a loud *pop*. "Well, let's go find your clerk." She patted the bench.

Without a safety strap, Dime at least tied a pair of rope handles through the frame.

Lifting up, they moved out toward the city wall. Dime felt a slight sense of liberation that she no longer cared if anyone saw them as the towers passed by. Maybe she should care, but one could only care so long before xe realized xe couldn't. They'd already been given a sense of who she was, she might as well give them the accurate one too.

Once they left the city, she did avoid the villages, staying over the open plains. No need to scare some villager who might not even follow city news.

The nightlight shone down on the broad expanse of Sol's Reach as they flew across it. A pack of wolgs ran across a patch of red soil, the color muted in the nighttime light. She wondered about them, for the first time.

"Why do you think they run in groups?" Dime asked. "Wolgs, I mean. It's as if they are a family. Or friends. But they are animals, so by definition they don't have family or friends."

"The newts do," Rock said.

"I know. We're begrudgingly developing some sort of exception for the newts, who are admittedly more intelligent than any animal I've seen, but once that wall is broken down, where does it stop? Or should there never have been a line in the first place?"

"Why can't it stop at the newts? I haven't seen other animals that communicate and form relationships like they do. It's a lot like pyrsi, really. Pyrsi plus newts. I can get with that."

She thought about it. "There is a little kita that has followed Tum around since Tum was very young, well since they both were. She calls her Agni. And, now that I'm thinking of it, anyone who has seen Agni interact with the kids would not consider her incapable of relationships and communication. At some level. If a kita, why not a squip? Yet look how we talk about all of them. Even at that rally, the fairies were talked about like animals, like they were buzzers or something. Fairies are certainly not buzzers and should never be spoken of as such, but on a different level, why would buzzers not deserve our respect? Isn't that the same way we dismiss the newts? Simply because they aren't pyrsi?"

"Why do you talk about animals so much?"

"What are you talking about? I really don't. It's just when I do even a little, pyrsi zone in on it."

"Didn't you do something with peckbeaks? Back at the IC? Someone told me about it and I was like, oh, D."

She glared at Rock. "There is never a reason to be like, 'oh, me' but anyway, yeah, that's right. I didn't think of it as an animal thing at the time. It was just Maintenance was pruning all the trees around the complex, both for looks and to reduce their sap content so pyrsi weren't getting sap on them while taking a break in the gardens. But the peckbeaks drill for the tree sap, and like I was saying, the sap doesn't grow as thick if the branches are pruned. So the peckbeaks started, er, pecking around the trees more bells than normal, then that annoyed pyrsi. Everyone was trying to propose ways to shoo the peckbeaks away so they'd be less irritating."

"Of course you took this on as a cause." Rock's mouth had upturned a touch, enough that Dime could see it from her side.

"See, that's exactly what I don't get. Why do these things have to be a cause? If birds like trees, can't we just leave trees for them? The towers are for pyrsi. Now the gardens are for pyrsi. Then the plains are for pyrsi. The forest. Where is everyone else supposed to go?"

"This is exactly why I love you," Rock murmured. Flushing as if she'd misspoken, she stammered a bunch of words that ended with something about Intinpalo. "I mean, he's terrible, but I can't help being curious what he thought. Your father did make him look like a turd. So, where did you say they hang out? You were telling me about it? We can see if he got back safely. Look, I don't like him, but I'd hate to find out he had an issue getting back. He was older than my agent's guidebook. Let's go see him."

Intinpalo? They'd been talking about Neimano and Agni and where had Rock brought the Eoch fairy into this? She steered a bit, avoiding a taller plateau. "We just saw him tonight; he's probably still sleeping off those two long flights."

"Nah, a guy like that would go back to the others. He'd have to tell them something, even if it was cryptic. I bet he practically lives at the Risers place. I know Eochs like him; they don't like being alone. And the night is well underway—it has to have been at least ten bells since he left. Or more? My guess, he crashed outside the city, woke up, flew back to the Heartland and at least stopped by before going home again. So what is this place again? You made it sound like a huge bar."

"Uh, sure. I was saying that their casual meeting place is actually rather grand. You can tell they are all high-class, which in Fo-ror culture means they are allocated a lot of resources, because what they do is considered important."

"It's complete absurdity." Rock made a *kaa* sound. "You tell me what is more important than cleaning toilets. Fo-ror and Ja-lal alike, paynotes or allocations—I don't care. The pyrsi who clean toilets should be draped in jewels and carried around on cushioned litters. Any society that doesn't get that is not yet right with Sol."

Rock was all over the place. Weren't they talking about the peckbeaks? Dime was trying to concentrate on flying a bench, something Rock seemed to forget. "You know, I got a lot of hassle for that peckbeak campaign. Pyrsi called me silly, said I didn't understand Sol's ways."

"I think we should go to their bar."

"What?" Dime turned around and they lurched mid-air, each grabbing their rope handle as Dime quickly adjusted the bench. Knowing they were a fair ways above the ground, though not as high as she'd gone strapped into her old chair, she vowed not to get distracted again.

"Whoop! Got that under control? Yes, I'm saying we should go to their bar. You only live once, right? I am so tired of all of this. Those Risers piss me off. Let's go there and at least make one of them buy me a fairy ferm."

That made no sense. "You have lost all reason."

Rock didn't answer.

"Fine. We'll stop by. Quickly! We are actually on a very important mission here."

"It'll take the edge off. Besides, I'm not saying we start a panic. I don't think we will. I agree with you; everything I've read says they rely on their status. They are against the Violence in a hypocritical haven't-thought-that-through way, but it's not like they'll attack us. At worst case, they'll huff and puff for a marshal and we'll just leave. But they won't, because they'd be embarrassed and they won't like bringing the Seats' eye to them. So we'll just slip in agent-style, get someone to buy us a drink, then go."

"Just don't say 'buy'."

"Ah, right. And I'm the expert. We'll talk around that, then. Still, there's got to be a way to do it."

While Dime couldn't believe they *were* actually doing this, a bell or two later, she wound the bench in through the maze of thick branches, and eked it onto an empty balcony at one end of the structure. "Is this really about his safety?" Rock was a caring pyr, but she clearly hadn't liked the intruding Intinpalo, nor what he stood for. She stopped. "Ah. You're just curious if my father got to him."

"Honestly. A little."

Rock showed no fear at all as she put her hands in her pockets and strolled into the main hall of the Risers' meeting area. It had a much different look in the nighttime, as instead of streams of light and the view of waving branches, the soft glowstones framed the space, placed on each vertical beam of the broad structure, and shielded so they shone down onto the floor. A gentle rain had started to fall, and, used to stone towers with their tops far above, Dime noted how pleasant the soft noise of the rain against the wood roof was.

The room was fuller than she expected it to be. A table surrounded by fairies fell silent. Rock didn't.

"Yallo. I'm Fe'Rock, a Ja-lal from Sol's Reach. Kind of an implied bet thing we've got going on here, and I was hoping one of you would gift me a ferm. We can chat. Two rules: No one says anything weird about ruling my home, since I'm not into it. Second, no Ja-lal are inferior because I'm literally right here. Tavern rules; you can understand that."

Slowly, a thin fairy wearing a chunky yellow necklace raised xyr hand. "I will?"

"Got a seat for me?"

As they scooted over to let Rock in, Dime recognized that she was being virtually ignored, except for a few pyrsi staring from across the hall. The table was soon fully engaged with Rock, and then others gathered around. Finally one older pyr, an awkward expression on xyr face, brought Dime a goldferm. Xe held onto another.

"Thank you," she said.

Xe stared down at her hair. "I heard you're a Fo-ror."

"It's complicated," Dime said.

"Yes, but is it true? Have you become a . . . Ja-lal?"

Dime turned to the pyr, recognizing xe didn't understand, but feeling exhausted from having to explain it again and again. Of even being asked to. Maybe Nafat did need that center; just get an expert to run it. "Forgive me if this comes across as direct," she said. "But if I have to define myself in your terms before you can interact with me, then you are communicating your own identity much more than you are trying to understand mine."

"*Huh?*" the pyr said, before taking a huge swig.

"Where's Intinpalo, anyway?" Rock asked rather loudly. "I thought he might be here, about now. Must not be, then?"

Dime snapped around, and realized that the pyr next to her did also.

The room fell into a chilling silence.

"You don't . . . know?" One pyr said it, and others cut their eyes over nervously. "He came back rambling about . . . your sort. Talking about their towers as if he'd been there." Everyone turned to Rock, and it was clear they weren't going to quote what he'd said.

Then a stocky pyr spoke up from the back corner. "The joke's over; might as well tell the brute. It was harmed hilarious. He's lost his mental capacity, is what. We told him so, patted him on the shoulder, and made sure he knew we'd be discussing new leadership shortly."

Rock downed the rest of the ferm and looked up at Dime. Dime knocked hers back—something she wouldn't normally do—and sat it on a table. "I'm sorry," Dime said, looking directly at Rock. "You were right all along."

Before the others could figure out what they were up to, they ran across the room and to the balcony, Dime not wasting a single stride before lifting the padded bench upward and getting out of sight.

"That might not have been my best idea," Rock admitted. "Once

I remembered they were probably all well-practiced at valence, drinking ferm, and full of high-class entitlement. Curiosity got me. Not the last time." She exhaled with some drama.

"Was the drink good?" Dime's had been rather light, but it looked like Rock had something else.

"Frankly, it was excellent. Second-best I've had tonight. You know, that whole hall was really lovely. The architecture itself was a work of art, didn't even need the smaller pieces hanging around. So much talent and beauty in one place. Think if they spent their time on understanding the world rather than defining it."

Dime was glad the rain hadn't lasted long, and she wiped the drops off of her hair as Rock took out an artstick and touched up her costume tattoos. The complex entrance was familiar to Dime now, and even in the dark, she knew where to set down into the trees, well out of view. Together, they walked toward the edge of the trees, seeing the broad stone archway surrounded by guards, and the path beyond which led back through the stone face into the huge entryway. While the towering wall stretched out in both directions, to the right there were a few smaller groves of trees eventually leading to scruff, and on the left the stone face slowly curved backward, leading to the hills where some of the complex's outdoor facilities were.

"You suggested you had a plan?" Rock said. Her voice sounded tenser than Dime expected. She'd been so confident before.

"Sort of." She peered over at the entrance. "If we can get him called in. The guards can send someone to find him, but I don't think I can stroll on up this time and ask them. Any ideas?"

"Yep. We'll just ask them from here."

Dime gazed at her suspiciously. Obviously if they yelled from here, the guards would come over here to look.

"You've clearly never done theater. Ever seen a voice thrower?"

The performers? Sure, Dime had seen them. They talked with their mouths closed, and then moved something else, like a puppet, to distract where the sound was actually coming from. But that was less than an arm-length away, not across a clearing. Was Rock going to traipse up there with a puppet? She supposed she'd arrived herself once wearing a jingling mop. "Yeah, sure, I have."

"How do you say it? Tikinal?"

She nodded, still staring as Rock searched the ground, finally selecting a rounded hunk of stone. "I think they'd call him 'High Clerk'." Dime paused. "You know you have an accent, right?"

Rock rolled her eyes and pulled one of her sleeves back, exposing her softly muscular arm. She pulled the stone back against her armpit, staring intently at the outer archway. Bowing a little, she stood and propelled the rock at the top of the stone structure, where it bounced off, skidded past, and clattered along the pathway. As the guards all turned to look, she called out in a perfect imitation of a stuffy fairy. "Summon High Clerk Tikinal immediately. We need him here now, before firstlight."

With a huff, Rock flattened herself onto the ground, Dime joining her in shock. "Those are the words they'd use," Rock whispered. "*Summon* means call pyrsi to the complex. Also, I have many accents. Benefit of having enjoyed a turn or two in this place."

Dime peeked up just enough to see through the brush.

The High Guard at the entrance turned in several directions, finally shrugging, then said something to one of the other guards, who flew off. Dime and Rock backed up slowly, staying out of view of the front entrance but still just able to see if anyone drew near. They sat down in a patch of scruff. Tiny stems poked Dime's leg, and, grimacing, she shifted into a more comfortable seat.

"Hey, I got us something at Nafat's." Dime pulled the colorful tin from her bag.

"I saw that. Was wondering what was in it."

"Let's find out." Dime pried open the lid, expecting one of those cookie sets with the fancy shapes, or maybe a sticky cake, because those did last forever. Not having a terribly sweet tooth or great teeth, she was hoping for mixed softnuts. That would be perfect about now. She was surprised, instead, to see an assortment of colorful cubes with chalky textures.

"I'm underwhelmed," Rock said.

"I thought maybe cookies."

"I don't think he'd want cookie crumbs in his museum."

She had a point. "The crate looked full. Maybe he'd bought them on sight and didn't know exactly what was in them."

"Maybe he likes mints." Rock popped one in her mouth. "They're not bad."

"Here, you can have them." She'd told Nafat they were for Rock anyway, and Dime's stomach was not ready for a box of candy. Rock tucked the tin into her bag. They continued to watch the path, which for the most part, remained clear.

"We should name the bench," Dime said after a bit, feeling bored. "Any ideas?"

"It's a bench."

Well, that was no fun. "What about the carved roses? We could call it Rosebench."

"Sure. Rosebench it is."

They sat a while longer, Dime not sure what to do with the silence. "So this is old school," she finally said, watching a few fairies leave after their shift, but not seeing any enter. "You and me, staking out a place for an interview." The leaves rustled above them.

Rock didn't answer. Dime started to worry something was wrong, when her friend suddenly blurted out, "I feel awful about what I said earlier. The part about loving you. How are we supposed to have a friendship when I throw that sort of thing at you when you're just trying to talk about birds? I'm really happy to see you again. And you and Dayn have made an amazing family. I've just grown old and weird."

Rock turned to more of an angle, holding her knees tight against her chest. "You never even said goodbye. You never dropped me a note. You were just . . . gone. And I feel ridiculous now talking about this, like I'm some smitten Aoch. I'm sitting here, endangering our friendship, because I can't control my harmed-off mouth. I just want to promise you that I'll fix it. Now. And I'm sorry."

Oh. What was Dime supposed to say to that? She supposed she should say something. Her heart sort of turned over in her chest, and, well, she knew why. This wasn't any surprise. Dime had felt a little of the same way. Rock had shown up out of nowhere, older, funnier, and *more* beautiful than Dime had remembered her. Not to be superficial, or maybe beauty wasn't even the right word. She exuded warmth, and strength. She made Dime feel like things would be better. Like something had returned to her that had been lost.

She couldn't say any of this. For many reasons. She couldn't say none of it either.

Rock forced a smile, though not looking at Dime. "Oh, Sol, D. It's enough. I've apologized. There's nothing more to say. If you're willing to be friends, or if you'd rather not, I understand and there's no hard feelings. I'll still help where I can. I'll work with the Free Winds if I can't work with DC. Batu is amazing; we've connected. She could get me in the right group."

Dime spoke slowly. "You've hurt nothing in our relationship. I will be friends with you if you will be friends with me."

"I can't—"

She knew whatever Rock couldn't say, it wasn't that they couldn't be friends.

"I feel ridiculous."

Dime stared at her a long moment. "You are the least ridiculous pyr I have ever met." Rock shook her head. "No, really." She might as well go there. "Dayn once took ten full turns to build a mantle for the fireplace. The living area was a mess the entire time. I had to wipe wood dust off the tabletop with a wet towel just to enjoy a book." She stopped, not sure why the mantle had come to mind.

"That is actually ridiculous." Rock smiled, and it seemed more natural than before. "He seemed really great during our brief conversation. This isn't about that. You know that."

"I know. I actually think . . . he understands."

Her eyes clouded. "Understands?"

"He said . . . it was ok that I still had feelings for you and that he trusted me."

Rock spun around. "Wait, here I am making torn pants of myself for your amusement and whispering that I love you on our flying couch, and the whole time you told your spouse you still have the hots for me?"

"I did not say that I— Harm it, Rock, however you want to say it. Yes. I like you. You like me. I'm a one-spouse pyr and I love the one I have. And when you ran off in the woods, I— Harm's auncle, can we be friends or not?"

Rock tapped the ground. "Here's my proposal. Oh, that's not right. Here's my idea. We aren't going to like, have a hug moment because we already shared the flying chair so there's no point. But can we perhaps agree on a bridge or something and then—"

Dime couldn't look Rock's way, but she reached out her hand and held it next to Rock's. It was hard not to jump when she felt Rock's soft, bony fingers weave into hers. And they sat there, at the edge of the forest, quiet amongst the chirps and creaks with their fingers softly intertwined. And she held on a little longer. A little like she'd never left. And—

"Ok, that's good," Rock said, popping her hand away. "I'm over it now. Thanks for the talk. I pledge to stay friends, no more weird, and still the separate-chair and/or roomy bench contract."

Somewhere in the warm, and not-feeling-weird-at-all smile that they shared and the peace of the next take or two, there was a commotion of guards rising to their feet.

"Tikinal!" Dime said it aloud, but glanced over to see the fairy, with his sweeping robes and distinctive knot of hair, had already landed on the path's main loop and was walking toward the arch.

"Killbird, we were supposed to be watching for that," Rock whispered. "What sort of blurpball agents are we?"

"Are you a ch'pyr?" Dime hissed, scrambling to remember what she had planned to do.

"At heart!" Rock whispered. "Say something!"

"Brooms! Stink!" she called out in a high, chirpy voice, and whatever she'd meant to do, it was done so poorly that pretty much every guard craned in their direction. As Tikinal scrambled to regain the guards' attention, Dime and Rock pressed flat into the ground with Rock's eyes wide in humor or scolding or who knew.

A take later, the guards were back in position, if looking a little antsy, and Tikinal had launched back into the sky.

"I see why they put you at a desk," Rock said.

"If they hadn't, I wouldn't know the High Clerk."

"Got me there."

And when their eyes met, something became right.

Interlude

Dot loved when the brick fell right into place. No taps, no wriggles—he barely had to scrape the mortar even. If things kept going this well, he'd be done with the job before Sol rose, and maybe he could even make it over to the club to help knit blankets for the new arrivals.

It was hard to meet the arrivals sometimes, but that wasn't their fault so he tried not to let them see his discomfort. Usually it was their first hemsa—once you left Lodon it was harder to get more—and like any new tattoo, the redness hadn't subsided by the time they showed up here in Dales.

Dales was on the maps as an "outlaw town", Dot had heard, so that explained why pyrsi just showed on right up. Dot smiled when they arrived, trying not to note the red in their eyes that surpassed the red to their skin. "You can go back and visit," some pyrsi would reassure them, but Dot never did. He knew how hard it was to go back to a place where pyrsi would only see you for one thing. One thing, in his case, that he'd done cycles and cycles ago.

He regretted it. In his case, he'd spoken harmfully to a friend he'd met at the playcourt for having an eye that didn't work the way other pyrsi's did. His Ma-ma used to say when they passed through the lowcity that some pyrsi weren't meant to make ba'pyrsi. She didn't say it in public of course, but Dot heard her saying it to Da-da in the toothcar. And so he'd told the other Aoch, while they were arguing over careers or something, that he shouldn't have been born. Turned out, the other pyr was from a real high-class family and young Dot was turned right in, and given the hemsa for being an abuser.

After his mother started treating him about the same way—for he was now permanently marred and embarrassing in her eyes—he left Lodon, and went on his way until he found a home, here in Dales.

Pyrsi here had talked him through it. Explained that all pyrsi were different, and that commenting on a pyr's body in such a way was the Violence, especially the way he'd done it. What he'd done was a form of supremacy, and put that way, Dot had nearly withered into the ground. They were right, you know. And what he'd done felt . . . awful.

He'd changed so much since then. Just the memory of what he'd done now made his stomach wrench. But it couldn't be changed. Time didn't work that way.

The message he always had for the new arrivals was that whatever they'd done, it was possible to change. It was possible to be a better pyr. And if they'd lost their loved ones from before, they'd find new ones, here.

Harm bucket! He'd gotten so distracted by the old thoughts, that brick had set down crooked. He went to tap it, but chipped off a whole corner instead. Muttering, he pulled the brick out and wiped it down, setting it to the side of his lamp. That one was now for projects at home. Always a silver lining, like his mother had said.

The next one went in real smooth.

As far as he knew, his mother was well in Lodon, and his siblings visited her often. Pyrsi sometimes asked if he'd go back. Here, pyrsi treated him well. Knew he was a good enough pyr. And they all had their own hemsa too. Everyone had done something, and everyone had changed. And grown. There, they'd only see the mark. They'd only shake their heads at the sort of pyr that he was. When they didn't even know him.

Just wasn't worth it.

Funny he was thinking all this. He sometimes got this way thinking about the new arrivals. He'd better concentrate. After all, it was a lovely night, the bricks were laying in nice—everyone puts one in funny every once in a while—and he thought he'd have plenty of time to get to the club.

Content, he started to sing.

Act 2

Treetops

Tikinal was waiting just where Dime had hoped he'd be. They'd approached the location on foot, leaving Rosebench hidden in a brushy patch. To avoid the risk of being seen, Dime and Rock had taken a large swath around the complex, staying to denser groups of trees and avoiding the sparser sections of green and brown.

Having a feeling Tikinal would not wait along the hedge near the unpleasantly fragrant compost, they'd walked instead to the hill where he and Dime had their last conversation, what now seemed a very long time ago—though it wasn't really. The lumber storage area had a soft scent of cut wood that made it a pleasant place to converse, while large stacks of fallen tree trunks protected anyone from being seen beyond them.

Tikinal struck an imposing figure, even in the dark of the trees and the shadow of the lumber stacks. Not tall, but distinct in his smooth robes and with the silhouette of the elaborate knot of hair above him.

"Sorry for the delay," Dime said. She almost explained why they hadn't flown, then realized Tikinal didn't yet know that she could— at least, not to her knowledge. "You weren't summoned by the Seats; I assume you know that? It was us."

"Yes, surmising that, I had a bit of cover up to do."

Dime couldn't tell from his tone whether he was irritated by this, or proud of how he'd handled it.

"I apologized for my outburst on the way down; said I'd almost dropped my nice pen. Then, since presumably I'd been called *inside*, I pretended one of them had just handed me a note and I had to leave to address it instead. Since there are always secrets, no one dared question this, and everyone figured it was someone else who had given me the note. Then I told them to keep tight to the entrance, as I was concerned that someone might try and gain entrance to Chambers with such an important session impending. Also, hello?"

"Yes, hello." Dime tried to smile. "I know this is awkward. Again. Can I just catch you up?"

The clerk's eyebrows raised, only slightly, but easier to see since he grew hair across them.

"I'm who I said I was when we first met," Dime began, "and everything I said in the complex was also true, though incomplete. Hopefully Layanie's not too mad at me?" Tikinal held rigid, so she continued. "I'm a fairy by birth. Neimano had my wings removed in some wicked scheme to take down the Ja-lal, and Ferala knows about it."

Tikinal drew in a harsh breath, but Dime went on. "However, turns out you don't *need* wings for valence, and I've learned how to use it. My valence is powerful, but mostly because of this diamond"—she pulled it out then dropped it back into her tunic—"that Neimano gave someone who was likely coerced into helping him, so that pyr secretly gave it to me. I fly around on chairs using valence, which is how we got here this time."

She extended an arm in Rock's direction. "This is my best friend, Fe'Rock. She's a soly—a term I've heard used for Ja-lal—and we both used to work for the Circles. She's the one that was in the diamond cages several turns ago; she was there looking for me. You can trust her. Our careers both met less glorious endings, and here we are just hoping for peace. If we can ever return to some sort of normal life,

I'd like to run a music school, and—" Awkwardly, Dime didn't know what Rock wanted to do.

She glanced at Rock, expecting to see her annoyed, but instead she looked rather . . . content.

"I haven't got that far," she said. "Not something too different, though. We'll see."

Tikinal's expression had shifted between shocked and appalled, and then landed on a stunned stare, but he recovered quickly. "Dime, it's nice to see you again—and well, after our last encounter. Truly. You do complicate my clerking, but thus far I have managed it. Burgess Rock, lovely to meet you. I suppose I should address the entire list of what you just said, but I'll admit, I'm interested in the music school. It's a very . . . Ja-lal way of thinking, you know."

"It is," Rock agreed. "I've studied the Fo-ror a bit and 'what do you want to be' is not something that Fo-ror ch'pyrsi are asked, is it?"

Tikinal winced.

"Ja-lal ch'pyrsi are asked that very young," Rock continued. "Usually it's in the context of what a parent's done, but there is often a suggestion of trying something new, something considered better. Do you know what my mother called it? 'Flying for the treetops.'" Rock shook her head. "I always thought she meant like a bird."

Dime was surprised to hear Rock mention her family. Now that she thought of it, she hadn't mentioned them at all these last turns, and Dime couldn't remember much from before. That didn't always mean something; sometimes pyrsi who lived in the city had a whole family in some outlying village, and while they were apart, they didn't always bring them up.

"I love music," Tikinal said, gazing wistfully upward along with Rock, as if they were both watching a bird together. "While I would never wish such a thing, many times I've considered what my life would have been like being born into a family of musicians. Or joining one. I could have done that. Some forms of music have an equivalent class level to administration. But I fell in love with a writer." He sighed. "Ma'Anathatu. Who is often grumpy when I get called in during a game of Treetops." He smiled at Rock. "Here, it's a game."

Dime perked up. "Wait, that's the game you got me, isn't it? You know, before." She turned to Rock. "I gave it to Ador. It's *beautiful*. An elaborate wood structure that moves into position as the case opens, and little carved squips and green ledges, like a tiny forest. He and Luja worked out a set of rules just for something fun to do, but I know they'd love to play it properly. Tikinal, maybe you'll show them sometime." Rock was moving her eyes as if in signal. What was she— *Oh*. "Please apologize to Anathatu for me! I didn't mean to interrupt the game."

Tikinal burst into laughter. "He would like you! But ... I'm thinking now about Ja-lal music. So much of our rhythm and melody derives from the cadence of the forest and the movement of our culture. It's the first thing we teach a ch'pyr. Ja-lal music must be different."

"It is," both fe'pyrsi said in unison. Rock gestured for Dime to continue.

"I've heard fairy music, and it's a lot different." She loved hearing the way Tikinal described it; she viewed music in similar terms and would love to discuss it with him.

"It's not as if we just have one style," he cautioned.

"Right," Rock added. "But she's saying even so she'd never heard anything like it."

Tikinal gazed ahead, as if he were watching reality return. "But we will not play Treetops together, and really, you should not be here. Though, I see you avoided breaking your pledge to Seat Layanie by not entering the complex directly." He glanced back in the direction of the long hedge. "I'm glad you had that discretion. I am ... concerned about the state of things."

"About Neimano, what happened in the forest." The air around them had shifted, and Dime recognized they needed to get to it before she got the clerk in any trouble. "He was injured: a consequence of his own making. So was Ulkanet."

"Ah." Tikinal nodded slowly. "Ulkanet has not been back. Neimano made the error of involving a group of burgesses he encountered, who rushed to alert the High Guards of the emergency."

Dime remembered he'd heard Neimano's accusation—that she had caused the injuries. Yet, he'd still trusted to meet her here. Alone. That was nice.

"As a consequence," Tikinal continued, as if not wanting to discuss that piece, "Seat Neimano was hurried into Sha's Infirmary, where he fell in and out of consciousness for a long while. He'd released himself from their care just before your recent arrival, a dilemma healers often face when treating those with, in Seat Neimano's case, nearly absolute authority. Yet his weakness in your presence was a cause for alarm, and I escorted him back for a brief examination. However, because of the spread of rumors surrounding the nature of his condition—he told many pyrsi to pursue the brute who attacked him—he is now required to stay there. With the High Seat's blessing."

Rock snorted. "Ha! Pyrsi are worried he caught a Ja-lal disease, and so you've arrested him?"

"It's not arrest. It's confinement for medical concern."

"*Pfft.* Still, that's great. Look, I'm not bending on this arrest thing, but don't tell me that's not funny at least for now, and quite directly, I'm glad to hear he's been kept out of trouble." She stuck her hands in her pockets. "I, er, got tied up myself, and—"

"I'm not going to keep rehashing what we should have done." Dime said this to Tikinal as poignantly as she could. "But my sense is Neimano still holds a threat to peace. Whatever has been done, whatever hasn't been done, we must step forward now and do what must be done."

"What do you want from me?" Tikinal said, his voice low. His robes swayed in a slight breeze that whistled through cracks in the lumber.

"I want to know what else Neimano might have planned. I want to know why many of his victims have died or been harmed. I want to know what I am not seeing in all this."

Tikinal collapsed back onto a log, something Dime figured he didn't normally do given the fine fabric of his robes. He hadn't commented on the idea of victims not surviving, which to Dime meant maybe he'd known some of this but wasn't comfortable discussing his source.

"I am more worried than I've ever been," he said. "I'm not their age, so I don't have the full background. I wasn't there when Neimano first held Ninth Seat. I was only a ch'pyr during the curse, and I was kept away from most of it even then.

"By the time I was selected as High Clerk, this was all a secretive past, just as it is to you now. Over time, I suspected there was much more to Neimano and Ferala's tumultuous relationship. To Neimano's toxicity and Ferala's fear. Snippets here and there. Hints. Worries."

It was not a secretive past to Dime; she was living its effects. But she knew what Tikinal meant and did not interrupt as he continued.

"In an odd sense, they have kept each other from acting. Neimano lords Ferala's mistakes over him. And Ferala breathes the hint of threat: that whatever it is that Ferala could expose, it would destroy them both. And by that, I mean destroy their status of course.

"The spans are racing quickly now. Everyone feels it. Whatever timer Neimano set, or we all set in our inaction, it is close to expiring." He closed his eyes. "Ferala and I have . . . differed on approach."

The rest went without saying. Ferala was High Seat of the Heartland. Tikinal was a clerk. Even suggesting their disagreement was farther than Dime had heard from fairies other than Intinpalo.

She respected Tikinal a great deal and empathized with his conflicts. Yet she couldn't stand here and continue to condone the reverence, that same lack of challenge that had brought them here today. "I've decided something, in all this." She glanced at Rock, who nodded her on. "Disproportionate power—status as you call it— should always be given, never taken. When someone is given power over another, xe has trust. Xe has responsibility. If one chooses to honor this power for the benefit of all, great things may occur. But when power is taken, to honor that power is only to honor theft. The taking of power is always the Violence, whether done through blades or lies."

Both Tikinal and Rock cringed in unison, one in front and one to her side.

Dime did not stop. "Our societies struggle with the idea of telling truth to power, as if this is disrespectful, when it is not. Telling truth to power respects that power, enables it. But moreso, we should recognize when power is false. When it should not be honored." She sighed. "I know it's all oversimplified, but we must continue to have these discussions, to act on what we believe."

The clerk held still, his face tight.

"What is it? What do I need to know?"

Slowly, Tikinal withdrew a pad from his satchel, and drew a crude sketch—Dime could see it was a map. After folding the sheet, he stood and handed it to her. "The paper shows you where to go. Destroy it when you arrive."

Dime nodded.

"It is a location where you may speak to the one pyr who might be able to help you best. What Ferala knows, xe will know. What else xe knows, I am not sure. This was our best effort. Our best compromise. There is a token needed to signal xem. I don't have it. That's all I can say. One question, if you would. Your friend, is he well? Does he have a role in this?"

She realized he meant Uchitar. "He's recovering; thank you. No specific role—we just care about him."

"I will think on his continued recovery." Tikinal, who a take ago had worn such a warm smile, looked tired. Uneasy. "It is volatile here, and I must get back inside. As for you, I would stay away from the complex. Stability is tenuous, and since I don't know which way the dishes would fall, I would not disturb them quite yet. Rock, it was my pleasure to meet you, even so strangely and briefly." He nodded toward her, the way Sala might acknowledge a guard. "I hope you both find what you seek." He paused a rather long time, and Dime knew that he was considering something, so she waited.

"If I can help in additional ways, you may let me know," he finally said.

She knew what that meant. Not what it meant but what it *meant*. What it would mean to a Fo-ror to sound disloyal to their Seats, to the very structure of Sha. She could have told him that forced loyalty was the Violence, that surely Sha's way was to be good to each other. But this wasn't her culture, and he hadn't asked about hers. Tikinal was older than her, though not much, and he had lived a uniquely insightful life. If he was making this decision, then he already knew.

"Thank you so much," Dime whispered instead.

"I've told you enough to be arrested for treason." He was almost talking to himself.

"I will honor that as best I can."

They were both glad to see that Rosebench was just where they'd left ver. Dime didn't want to use valence again until they'd left. So heaving a little as the base snagged on the rough brush and roots, they dragged the bench back out between the trees, a spot with full canopy overhead. Sitting down together, Rock unclipped her flask and pulled out a wrap of crackers.

"Cracker?" she asked, holding one out.

Dime crunched it between her teeth, before digging out her own flask of water to help with the dry flakes sticking to her mouth. "That was conversation sabotage," she said. "Good crackers though." They were clearly made by Batu, or at least made wherever Batu got her groceries. "Is that lavender?" she asked, parsing the taste lingering on her tongue.

"It is," Rock crunched out through a mouthful of crackers. "I've become a fan." Rock stopped talking, seeming to realize that even with lavender accents, the powder of cracker residue escaping from her mouth was a bit unappealing for a Gamh. She pulled a napkin from her pocket, covering her mouth. "So what's on the paper? A map?"

Dime opened it and squinted to make anything out, though even here in the dark, she was careful to keep it hidden from anyone who might be peering from a distance, through a device, or perhaps with valence—who knew anymore. Once she had the basics, she folded it back up and into her pocket. "Yes. It also specifically tells us not to fly all the way there. There's even a little × for where we should land."

"He's quite thorough."

"He's their top clerk."

"Fair. Well, we should go?"

"Should we rest first?" It had been a long night, and since finding Rock up in the foothills with Jaza, they'd only slept once properly, back at Batu's. It wasn't healthy to keep up like this. Dime considered how far away they were from that room in the hills, from the length of concealed rope.

"We should," Rock considered. "But I say we go anyway. I'm alright. Done worse."

"Yeah." Dime felt the same way. There'd been a tremor to Tikinal's tone that was agitating inside her. For now, they'd keep going.

Moving up and then away from the complex, they stayed atop the canopies, catching glimpses of the canal structure that formed the basis of Tikinal's map. She swerved a few times, trying to stay away from high-class residences or gathering areas that peeked through the leaves and up into the night. After passing a group of ponds, Dime set down where Tikinal had recommended. To her amusement, it was not far from an out-of-use compost hill, though at least it was old enough that the odors were muted. The shape of it rested funny, perhaps as though the land had been mined here, then refilled. Trees worked to grow through the top of it, some angled oddly.

"I see why he thought our bench would be safe at the ×," Rock muttered. "Left that marking off." She patted the bench. "Sorry, pal. I'm taking my bag though. Not many places I'd trust leaving it." Rock hoisted the bag up and over her back, looking to Dime for the way to start walking.

By the map, this was an outer ring of the city, and unlike the bustling trees of central Pito, Dime felt fairly comfortable here, wandering through the dark forest paths. After Rock took a hard trip over a root and clutched at her lower back, Dime grew concerned and called a small stone into her hand, letting it glow just enough to light their way. Maybe she wasn't supposed to signal their presence with valence or a traveling light, but she wasn't going to let Rock get hurt. She glanced up and around; they seemed to be alone.

Dime still wasn't used to walking in any type of forest; the wafting layers above were so fundamentally different from the sharp lines and clear skyviews of Lodon. Yet the darkness of this uninhabited section sometimes reminded her of a tent made of black veils, a dream place that couldn't be real.

The location marked on the map was unmistakable—a huge, ancient tree with a hollowed-out core, all leaning to one side. Swarms of bugs swirled up and around the trunk, grazing on the soft moss which grew against the dead remnants of the wood. Here, the smell was also not pleasant. She imagined this kept away any curious ch'pyrsi, who otherwise might have turned it into some sort of fort. That's what Dime would have done, anyway.

Since they were here, and there was nothing left to see on the paper, Dime honored Tikinal's request and lit the sheet aflame. She used a little valence to push cool air around the falling embers, to make sure no sparks fell against the old, insect-covered wood.

"So now we chant something?" Rock had her hands on her hips, leaning back.

Dime chuckled. "Pretty much! It said we set the token down here, I suppose on this ledge. Then we step out of sight."

"What a weirdo."

"Rock!"

"Well, please. If xe's listening, xe's not going to argue that. Set your token on the dead tree then step away? Anyone who doesn't understand that is maximum weirdo doesn't deserve the honor of being known as one. Right, secret pyr?" She glanced around into the surrounding trees. "Also, we don't have the 'special token'. And . . . our friend . . . didn't have the token. Got a token on you?"

"Uh, no?" Dime hadn't really understood the whole token bit. Like an entrance card, she supposed? She still had her Circles ID, but was pretty sure that wouldn't do.

"If you want, I could carve a little statue of myself offering the Soldown and see how xe takes that."

Hopefully the secret pyr wasn't too sensitive. She wondered if this was Rock's strategy to playing realms. Except, she played the Ambassador. What sort of Ambassador move was this?

Dime suddenly knew what token to use.

Unhooking her necklace, she set it into the empty space. A chubby kitapiller started to crawl toward it, then turned away. "Let's go," she said.

Together, they walked back into the trees, out of sight of the hollowed trunk. Dime could sense the diamond resting there; she'd sent a little extra valence into it, as she'd done at the beginning of the night to find Rock. As time passed, the diamond stayed where she'd left it. As Dime could figure, one of three things could have happened.

First, xe only responded to the correct token, or the diamond hadn't been what xe wanted. Dime didn't think this was the issue. Tikinal wouldn't have sent them here if he thought it was that unbending, and leaving her diamond unattended certainly showed she was serious.

Second, xe was deciding whether to answer their request. Dime had a hunch this was likely. And she didn't blame xem.

Third, the pyr wasn't there. Xe'd gone out to a show, or was fast asleep in a city home. Or xe was off living xyr secret life on a shift somewhere. Maybe even in the complex. Except, if xe was in the complex, it seemed Tikinal might have had a way to alert xem to return to this place.

"Let's eat," Dime finally said. She didn't want to leave without answers. If xe took too long, they'd get some sleep. They needed it.

Dime unpacked the remaining fresh food Batu had supplied them. The sandwiches held up nicely in the tightly wrapped paper, and the way Batu had layered in the sharp pretzel strips, they even still had some crunch, contrasting the luscious avo cream.

"We can't just stay with Batu forever, right?" Rock patted her stomach.

Dime laughed. It wasn't as if the thought hadn't crossed her mind. "I think we can probably swing getting invited over for a biscuit sometimes."

"I can live with that," Rock responded before finishing off her water flask.

"It moved," she blurted out. The movement of the diamond had jarred her, like being pulled by a wind.

Rock pushed the wraps into the dirt and clipped her empty flask to her bag. "So I guess xe's cool to see us."

"This way," Dime said. "Xe's leading us somewhere."

She was glad Rock didn't question how she could feel the diamond pendant when she couldn't see it. It wasn't like a sound one could hear, or a spot on a map. It was like knowing a friend had left a room and walked to another. Just—knowing it.

With that sense guiding her, they wound through the dark, shadowy trees. Still not seeing any homes or structures above them but only dense canopies, Dime wondered why this part of the forest was so unpopulated. She wasn't sure if this was considered Pito or outforest, but it wasn't so far away that there shouldn't be pyrsi here.

As they walked up to a cluster of trees, Dime stopped suddenly. "Look," she whispered. All around the base of the trees, moss-covered lumber rested in chaotic bundles, mixed with huge branches, char, and a few twisted pipes.

Dime could sense the diamond within them. "Xe's inside there. Not up in the branches." She said branches since there was no evidence of any structures still intact above.

Together, they scouted around the rubble, looking for something like an entrance. Should she lift the beams with valence? She didn't think so; the wood, overgrown with newer trees, had not been disturbed in a long time. It had a memorial-type quality to it, just a memorial that had not been tended to except by Ada-ji verself.

"I think it's in between," Rock said slowly. "Like, we can't enter here; we have to backtrack. The entrance isn't where the token is placed either; it'd be too obvious to search there. Somewhere between the two points. That's my sense."

Dime nodded. Would the entrance be through a tree? Through a door in a tree? Would it require flying to reach?

No, it couldn't require flying to reach, or Tikinal wouldn't have told them to leave the bench. Perhaps, though, that was a clue. Carefully, they retraced each step, Dime making careful note of her surroundings, working hard not to be distracted.

"So if xe wants us to find it," she said aloud in case it sparked any ideas for Rock, "it must be something xe's just opened for us. Xe wouldn't leave something obvious for a pyr to explore. And xe isn't waiting at it, either, so it's *findable*." She rested her hand on the rough bark of a trunk.

"What else did Tikinal say on the paper?"

"I don't think there was anything else; I don't know; I burned it."

Rock tapped her lip, then suddenly threw down her arm. "Look for a piece of paper. He told us, remember, the paper would show us."

But that had meant the paper he'd given them, didn't it?

When Rock was determined to find something, it was impossible to stop her. And she darted off, telling Dime to wait in place. Soon, she returned, beaming. "Found it. This way."

She pointed down at a sheet of paper bearing an unknown symbol. It was tacked into the joint of a small forest boardwalk, the sort built over a muddy patch.

Feeling around with her valence, Dime could see that a few of the boards were loose, like a, well, she still didn't know what to call a floor door. There was no handle, but unused to employing valence without her pendant, she stumbled a bit trying to open the panel, which rumbled under her hands.

"I'll get it," Rock offered. She tugged the boards open from one side, revealing a dark space below. "Now, destroy *this* paper." As before, the paper flared up and disappeared into ash.

They lowered in one at a time and closed the boards overtop. They stood, now, in stillness, the sounds of the forest muted. Only a faint trail of air, and deep, cool humidity surrounded them. The tunnel was pitch dark, but Dime still had the small glowing stone and she held it out. Her instincts urged her to leave the brooding space, but she was determined to continue on. She followed the pull of her diamond around a few bends and junctures. Neither of them spoke.

They stopped at a metal door tinged with what Dime recognized as diamond dust. It was propped open, and so the two walked in together.

"Please, take a seat," a smooth, unemotional voice said. Two low-backed chairs were set out in the middle of the room. Dime's glowstone lit up what looked to be a modest study, though an unseen barrier prevented the light from reaching the back of the room.

"I'll sit if you would show yourself," Dime said.

"I'm sorry; that's not possible," the voice replied. "I have trusted you, strangers, coming here, so I need to ask for some of that trust in return."

Dime met Rock's eyes, and in unison, they sat down.

"I'm Fe'Dime." With Rock's nod, she added, "This is Fe'Rock. Can I call you something?"

Xe hesitated. "I'd prefer not."

Alright, an *Agent X* then.

"So, why are we here?" As xe'd pointed out, they were the visitors. Fumbling for a moment with her valuables pouch, she pulled out the dice that Ador had given her just strides before the High Guards arrived. Amethyst and onyx, they almost glowed with darkness—with the reverse sense of light—in her hand. "I have learned that one never gets anywhere of value without taking some chances. Whether it's trying a new restaurant, leaving your career, or sliding underneath a forest boardwalk, there are things you won't find by staying on the path.

"I am prepared to be open with you," she continued, while carefully returning the dice to their home. "I have been to the Heartland before, looking for answers. I thought I found them. Yet there was an itch. A feeling something wasn't right.

"I know that Neimano had ten ba'pyrsi's wings removed, and I know he positioned them in Lodon for future activation as spies. If you've not yet surmised it or been told, I am one of those ba'pyrsi. I believe I was the first. But I still have questions. Why are so many of us harmed or returned to memory?" Her voice skipped, and she tried to calm herself. "Why did he send his guards to me if I had failed? When there were others out there, still capable of more? And most importantly, what is it that he plans now?"

A gloved hand reached out from the shadow, holding Dime's pendant. In the darkness of the room, it let a surreal light, bright but somehow incomplete. The hand tossed it into the air, and Dime used her valence to guide it, slowly and with care, back into her own hand. Reaching up, she fastened the chain around her neck and tucked the stone back under her shirt. Simultaneously, she felt the comfort of its protection and the discomfort of her reliance on it. Power returned to her fingers, as did her sense of control.

Yet the control here was not hers, here where Agent X set xyr own rules. In the dark room, still and quiet, Dime could only hear Rock's slow breathing. Agent X had heard her questions. Patiently, Dime waited for a response.

"Ferala has lived in shame under Neimano's manipulation." Xyr voice, still smooth, sounded affected, unnatural. "He never meant to be manipulated, but, young and confident, he felt trapped by the time he realized it. At first, you see, he underestimated how far Neimano would go. He sympathized with his anger, his frustration. Who wouldn't feel this way, experiencing the deep pain that the Fo-ror did at that time? All the complex felt it. Unable to blame Sha for the agony of watching pyrsi die, they reached for someone to be at fault. It wasn't difficult, with the fog of the Great War never really lifted.

"To this turn, no one knows where the curse originated. The theories of Ja-lal origin are weak, as no Ja-lal are known to have contracted the disease, even long enough to have been cured of it. And there is no evidence they are immune. The quarantines were swift and effective, and the outbreak was contained to the core of Pito."

Dime considered this. The rumor, as Ferala had recounted to her, was that someone had traveled to Sol's Reach and contracted the disease. How would they know this? She'd heard nothing that said the Underground had been impacted, if it had even been populated back then. Had there been an outbreak at the Crossing? It didn't sound that way. Could it be that the post-War isolation had been the only thing that had spared the Ja-lal this tragedy? Or were they immune? Or able to heal? They *were* better able to heal. And—to the core of Pito? Ferala had made it sound widespread.

The Agent was speaking. "When the rogue Seats met, they channeled this anger, bounced it between each other. Because the outbreak had been so close to the complex, they were all pyrsonally affected. Many of their friends and family had been taken. Ferala's only sibling. And not just taken—their last moments were known to be in agony and alone, since no family who wished to survive could stay to console them. Many healers stayed, pressed on. Soon it took them as well.

"As for the other three, it was not that their anger subsided, but their clarity resurfaced. Jolted by the cruelty of Neimano's plans, one by one they realized they could not react to death with more death. That healing would only come through love, not harm. And by the time Ferala understood that Neimano had not stopped, that he had continued on with his unspeakable plans—that Ferala had done nothing to stop him—he felt as broken as though he'd held the scalpel.

"He no longer wanted his power. He lost belief in a Sha that would allow a pyr such as Neimano and he almost left. Ferala lost himself in this shame. But the Heartland needed leadership, they needed solace. Or someone else might act. Someone else might follow Neimano and lead them further down a path toward War. Finally, Ferala found a way forward, by accepting that, as penance, he must stay in power, if only to keep Neimano in check—to prevent any further harm from occurring.

"For, at least, Ferala was a witness. He could expose what Neimano had done, with credibility."

Dime felt her hands shaking as the story continued, and she could not stop herself from interrupting. "Why didn't Ferala just stop him? Expose him then? Was he so afraid to lose his own power?"

The Agent paused. "Neimano loves power. He loves holding a Seat, as elevated now as Third Seat. Ferala thought, under his eye, he could prevent him from causing further harm. If Neimano were to lose his position, and Ferala along with him, he worried what lack of stability might result. Even locked in the dead caves, what further scheme might Neimano enact, enlisting those loyal to his cause? What revolt might occur from an already troubled pyrsi losing faith in their Seats? In Sha's designs? Could such an upheaval lead to the same return of War that he was trying to prevent? Would Neimano start his revolution more effectively from the outside? High Seat Ferala is not, as you say, one to roll the dice."

"They never are," Rock muttered. "Those comfortable with their power never like to risk it. Whatever the reason."

"I agree," xe said.

Dime had not had any sense from the shadowy figure what xyr position was on the Ja-lal. Xe'd not shown any reaction to Rock's presence, not annoyance, fear, disapproval. In fact, it was hard to read anything through a voice speaking in an affected tone through a dark shadow. Though grateful that xe seemed to be sharing openly with them, Dime felt a wave of irritation at the imbalance of being here, exposed, yet speaking to no one.

"You were not forgotten," xe said, out of nowhere, Dime felt, as she sensed that xe turned to face her. "There was even talk about retrieving the ba'pyrsi that had been sent away." The Agent's voice, which had remained steady, trembled just a bit at these words, and xe inhaled audibly. "Without wings, they were better suited to Ja-lal life. They had families, by then, futures. And no records to even bring peace to their families here, if their families here had even survived. Ferala decided it would be kinder to leave them be, and focus on preventing Neimano from harming them again. From harming anyone."

She felt no connection to these sentiments, only more irritation. Deep.

"So, who am I?" the pyr asked.

Dime straightened.

"No one. I was no one from the moment I agreed to assist. My task was to keep eyes on Neimano when Ferala could not. Like an alarm of woven valence in a corridor, that is my main purpose. If Neimano was no longer contained, I would alert Ferala. So, Ferala knew that Neimano had sent High Guards to summon you. He knew that you escaped. And now, he frets span by span without knowing when or if he should act, as he secretly uses all his influence and the last of his favors to keep Neimano in the infirmary a small while longer. For his protection, he says."

Dime did not consider Neimano sending his guards to arrest Dime to be indicative of his continued containment, but right now, she wanted whatever answers she could get.

"He was injured because he attacked us," Dime said. "The effects he caused returned back on him, not through my influence."

That was a bending of the truth, but it did not break, and Dime was determined to protect the newts from Fo-ror influence or retribution.

"We did not know all that happened."

Rock turned to watch her. She'd not been there in the forest to feel what Neimano had done to them, though she would have been if she hadn't have stormed off. Yet, Jaza had done something similar to them both. So, actually, Rock would understand.

"Neimano found me in the forest … with my children." She didn't really feel comfortable admitting to the stranger that her Ja-lal children were in the Heartland forest, but she needed xyr continued openness. Besides, they'd been there. Maybe Agent X needed to know that Neimano's attack on children was not some one-time thing. It was who he was. A hollow core, just like that huge tree outside. This was the pyr they'd enabled. Protected. For whatever reason. Maybe Ferala needed to know that.

"He attacked us, using some type of pressure to take our movement, leaving us just barely enough breath to stay, stunned in place. Ulkanet was with him, ready to tie us all up with your diamond arrest ropes." Even in the dark and silence, Agent X's discomfort was clear.

Realizing that the next part of the story could wander close to explaining that it was Stern Eyes who had attacked the fairies, she quickly skipped forward. "Neimano flew away and encountered a group of pyrsi returning from the centernight speech, at commons. Either they happened to see him injured or he told them, but either way he sent them after me, saying I had harmed him, when I had not. In fact, my Aoch child spent a good two takes stabilizing Ulkanet's wounds, at vis own risk. Ve left the scene with fairy blood on vis torn shirt—the same fairy who had threatened to tie ver with ropes. I am sure," she continued, annoyed at herself for returning to the scene of the attack and wanting to divert, "that at least one of those pyrsi would have justified the Violence against me had I not been able to leave. One was charging at me as I sped away."

In the long silence that followed, Rock offered her a little smile, though the soft light of the glowstone revealed the concern across her face.

"Ferala won't be able to keep him in the infirmary for long," Agent X said. "Neimano is livid and will not suffer the display of Ferala's rank. Soon he would force Ferala to call it what it is—arrest—or to let him free. I have been considering when to urge Ferala to greater action, and I fear this will be that time."

"I agree," Dime said. "On both counts. One, Neimano will not stay confined, either physically or under the idea that someone can control him. And whatever he planned to do, I think he will now do it."

The silence dragged on again, but if this pyr needed time to think, Dime could allow it. It was funny, she considered, how they'd let the pyr pose danger for more than two full epochs, and now it felt like even a turn could matter.

"I suppose you must know," xe finally said. "Neimano claimed a deep chamber; he's had it for as long as I can discern. It is within the diamond caves, in a restricted area. The room is heavily guarded by a net of valence and diamonds. If anyone approaches, Neimano would instantly know. For cycles, I've tried to learn more, but this one secret Neimano guards as if it is the sole secret. Anything I could do to learn more might have shown my hand, something I was not willing to risk without knowing what I could cause.

"I've learned this. Whatever is in there is something called a *weapon*. If you are not familiar, a weapon is an object designed to harm. In the War, both sides used objects to harm, both common and invented this way, these *weapons*."

Even the word upset her. *Weapon*. It was soft, and rounded, like a hug, but with a tiny punch inside. One word that held so much pain. She remembered her conversations with the High Seat and the Light, hints they had let slip. "The Ja-lal relied on blades and machinery, right? And the Fo-ror primarily used valence?" Dime could see Rock's eyes glowing, intent with interest.

"It's more complicated than that," xe replied, "but there is truth to your words. As to what weapon waits in Neimano's room, I can tell you I do not know."

Dime knew that tone of speech. Even from a seasoned agent, there were some tells that were difficult to hide. "But you have a theory."

Rock nodded, as if she'd been thinking the same thing.

"I learned once that it is his intent to use the weapon if his original plans fail."

If they fail. Then there was more. She'd thought so. This all seemed especially ironic, she thought, coming from a pyr in a secret room xemself.

"Further, I learned at one time, very long ago, vials were likely taken to the room. I don't know this for certain, I don't know if they are still there, and I don't know if they are related." Xe paused, and Dime knew not to interject. For a pyr living with this secret, she couldn't imagine the cost of telling it now.

"I believe the vials may hold the curse."

Dime gasped, covering whatever noise Rock had made. They both snapped around, staring at each other with the same unspoken words.

"It's related to his project in some way, I've discerned. It's from that era. And . . . after all . . . you're immune, right? If you're one of them, and you survived it? You could carry it; deliver it to anyone. You could infect the Ja-lal, perhaps catch them unawares."

She considered this, fighting back the revulsion that gripped her from the inside at the thought of such an intentional design. Layers of coldness must separate Neimano from the souls surrounding him. When she had considered him lonely, she had not fathomed the extent.

"Not just the Ja-lal," Dime stammered. "The elites of Lodon. That's where he placed us. In positions of power and influence. *Warmth of Sol.*" High-class lives weren't more important than any, but the level of calculation that had gone into Neimano's scheme chilled her. And eight other Seats had been there, had to have had a sense what he was capable of. What did they do, but leave him in power and hope to keep him bounded?

If there was a curse upon Ada-ji, it was that.

Dime considered the pyr's theories. "If Neimano thinks solies can be infected, then I doubt Neimano thought it was solies who infected them. Or there would have been an outbreak in Sol's Reach. I doubt even the Circles could keep that a secret. So it was always about more. He used pyrsi's pain."

Agent X did not respond.

"And if I'm immune because I've already had it, then I'm in a unique position to deliver it. I'm also in a unique position to . . . destroy it."

It was hard to use a word as harsh as *destroy*. Destroying another's possession was the Violence. Yet. Could there not be layers? One did not lament the destruction of a disease. One always had authority to the operation of xyr own body. Yet, the curse was in a vial, not a body. Did the curse have the right to exist? Was it impacted by Neimano's intent?

She remembered: This was not a natural dwelling. This was a substance saved, preserved by Neimano with the express desire to . . . to kill.

"I must destroy it," she said, seeing then that Rock was still watching her, intensity in her tight expression.

"We don't know much," Agent X said, softer now, as if xe'd forgotten to apply the artificially affected voice. "The medics did not survive. How it is transmitted, even. Must there be touch or would a cough suffice?"

Dime knew she should continue to ask questions, continue to absorb whatever information the pyr would give her. She was distracted by her anger.

Differing approaches were part of society's growth. A side effect of independent thought, a tenet she considered sacred. But a pyr who thrived on cruelty and self-enrichment being allowed to fester within a position of trust—she'd seen it before, it was part of why she'd left. Was she truly less powerful now? Or did she have more voice. More opportunity. Ferala could have done the same.

"If you do alert Ferala," Dime said, slowly, "which I think that you should, I ask that you also tell him you've already told us. I do not understand your arrangement, but I don't think it'll upset him that we're involved. Tell him . . . to buy . . . to *find* us time. I agree with what you are suggesting. If Neimano has been waiting for his plan to fail, it has failed. He will retrieve the weapon—these vials of curse—and he will use them. And who knows, *who knows* how many pyrsi he will harm along the way."

He had sent pyrsi to take Jaza. Nafat. Dime. He seemed to have avoided Olok for now. Dime had a sudden fear for Kolk, and there was still Cren, hidden somewhere in the mountains but perhaps known to Neimano . . . but either way—she had done what she could for the victims. She must get to this cave before Neimano did.

She stared back into the darkness that was Agent X. This pyr had given up xyr ability to live a normal life, perhaps—it was hard to say what sacrifice xe'd made. Yet she felt no gratitude. Xe'd known. For epochs, maybe.

Dime would leave this agent here and each of them would live with their own conscience, their own fate. A few words, only. A few slipped out.

"Tell Ferala it's hard for me to fathom the greatness of a society that would lock a pyr away for xyr addiction, but leave a pyr of such dangerous cruelty in power. To allow him such status."

Rock's chair creaked.

She expected more of a reaction from the agent. An argument perhaps. Even an intake of indignant breath. Instead, xe responded calmly, xyr careful voice back in place. "It is not just his status that is the issue. Power is always a web. Neimano has taken great care to ensure 'Sha's Traditions' are upheld—that those in power stay in power. If Neimano could lose his status, what about those whose status he has supported? What about the high class of Pito?"

Dime thought back to the Ja-lal parallels. For the Ja-lal, status was attainable. A dream shared by all. Yet she remembered how this all started: her willingness to walk away. Dime had disturbed that web as well, even if her footprints had been quickly swept aside.

She tried to focus. "Is there anything else we should know? Any other plans Neimano has? Anyone we should watch? Anything about getting to his chamber? Into the caves?"

Agent X seemed to be thinking.

"It is my sense that you are familiar with the feathered creatures of the Heartland."

Dime jolted. She surmised he didn't mean birds. Yet, if he already knew of her relationship with the newts, what would she have to hide?

"Yes," she answered. "I am familiar."

"They are students of the land. They know each stream, each bush. They know the tunnels beneath the land as well and have long passed that knowledge along."

Dime exhaled, her frustration growing. "I know being cryptic is sort of your thing, but it's just the three of us here and I think we've all put a lot on the table. Can you just tell me? Are you saying the newts would know a way into the caves? Other than through the complex?" Why didn't xe think she should go through the complex? "Oh. Neimano blocked the caves. Either way, I also told Layanie I'd ask ver before entering the complex again, and it would alert Neimano I was there. You're saying the newts could get us in."

She glanced at Rock, hoping for her reaction. "I dislike bringing them into this," she said.

"They're already in it," Rock responded. "They were pushed from their home as you were yours. We should at least give them the opportunity to help."

"But would they understand? Would they understand the danger?"

"We can talk about it," Rock murmured.

Except. "I thought they didn't like tunneling. That's why they never considered going under the net."

"They don't dig tunnels," Agent X explained, "but they will use ones that already exist. Many are pyr-made. There is a long history of Ada-ji, one we have neglected to pass along."

Not just neglected. Hidden. It made sense, though, on the tunnels. That's why the net was so expansive—it had to exclude them completely. If the netting just surrounded the city, or each village, they'd still find their way back in. Though, she thought with a smirk, thanks to Luja and Tum they'd found their way back in anyway. Well, then.

"That is all I have," xe said.

Dime sat, thinking what else to say.

"Before we leave," Rock said, surprising her, "do you have fresh water?" She held out her flask.

At first Dime thought, why would the pyr have fresh water in the hollows of some old ruin. Then, she considered, if this was the equivalent of a den, no agent would agree to hide in a place where the door could be sealed but without air, supplies, and adequate water.

Peering back into the darkness of the room, Dime almost burst out laughing. This pyr lurked in shadows, using valence to cloak xyr identity, and a false voice. What, was xe going to get up and reach for their flasks?

Rock's mouth was held tight, and she didn't look at Dime. "It's not a ruse," she clarified. "I had no sense that would work with you. I'd just feel safer heading out with some fresh water. After what you've told us, I feel less comfortable knocking on doors in Pito."

Her words brought Dime sadness, especially since she wasn't sure whether Rock meant that she could not be seen until they'd found Neimano's room, or whether she meant that it was harder to extend trust with the Violence on one's mind. No matter how many times this new thought entered Dime's mind, her upset did not fade. She hoped it wouldn't.

Either way, there was a logistical issue at hand. They were both out of water.

"Here." Dime reached for her flask and set it on the floor. Rock followed, leaning hers against it. "We'll close our eyes. I promise."

"I promise as well."

Trying to maintain a weighty countenance, they waited, eyes closed, until Agent X, again in the shadows, told them to open them. Picking up their full flasks, they returned each to their bags and rose to leave.

"Thank you for the information," Dime said.

Now Rock was biting her lip.

Dime felt like there would be parting words, or final wisdom, but not hearing any type of answer, they walked back down the corridor, and out through the opening above them. The sounds of the forest surrounded them. A warmbird flew by, its wings black against the tree trunks.

Standing, they watched as the boards of the pathway snapped back into place. With her diamond back on and just a *little* curious, Dime gently pried at them with her valence. "Locked."

Rock nodded. Dime could sense her relief, and felt it too.

Without warning, Rock collapsed into the leaves, bursting into stifled laughter. "That. Was. So. Weird."

For a moment, Dime too shed the weight of what Agent X had just told her, and she sat down next to Rock. Contagious, the laughter bounced back and forth, until neither could speak at all. Dime started to calm, then saw the actual tears rolling down Rock's face, and she lost it again, rolling back onto the ground.

Finally, Dime gathered the breath to speak. "I owe you an apology."

"I know!" Rock sat up. "I told you xe was a weirdo!"

"Remember when you asked for water? And we had to close our eyes?"

Again, they lost it, and Dime was glad that in a world filled with fear and worry and pyrsi capable of such cruelty, that laughter had not been taken from them. She allowed it to stay within her, easing the pressure that had built up, if only for a while.

"Oh, Sooooool." Rock scooted against a tree. "I hate to use the water so soon, but that got me." She took a swig, and then glancing at the flask with regret, clipped it back onto her bag. "So, I guess we're going to the Beds? For real, this time?"

Dime appreciated Rock putting it out there, as now she didn't have to avoid the implication that their last trip that way had been interrupted by Rock's departure. "I think so. Don't you? Our options are either wait and learn more, charge into the caves right away, or at least check with the newts first. Either way, we could act too soon. Either way, we could act too late." Then she remembered that Rock didn't know about the newts' valence, or that they'd been there during the forest attack, as she'd only mentioned her children. She wasn't going to say it here, so close to where the agent had been. Hey, if xe was listening in to the last part, that was on xem. But, she decided, she'd tell Rock before they got there. It felt . . . necessary.

Rock groaned, as she ran her boot back and forth in the dirt, creating an arc. "Newts. Let's ask the newts."

"Alright." Her neck felt heavy, and she thought again that it had been a while now since they'd slept. Determination was keeping Rock alert, but she could see the droop to her eyes. They were acting like Aochs; they should get some rest. "Do you, uh, do you want to sleep here for a while?"

Rock leaned her head lazily to the side. "You could really sleep after hearing what we just heard?"

Dime didn't bother to answer her. No. Of course she couldn't. If she was going to lie here in the dark forest and try to understand how a pyr could even imagine doing what Neimano had done, she would rather be on her feet, moving toward something that might stop him. It wasn't an argument that would hold forever, but it felt best for now.

"Let's get back to Rosebench," she said instead. "We'll skirt the city and find a stream to at least wash up."

Dime had to marvel a bit that the idea of using chairs to fly had been so novel and scary at first, but now it was effortless. To the extent that her friends were purchasing larger seats so she could take them as well. There might have to be some limits on that.

But for now, she and Rock found their way back, talking less, perhaps from the lack of rest or because they were both spinning on the agent's words. Relieved to sit back onto the firm cushions, with their bags nestled on each side, they flew away from the lopsided hill and the secretive ruins. Dime hoped she'd never see them again.

And as they curved around, staying high so as not to pass by winged fairies—flying was a whole different endeavor in the Heartland—Dime spotted a medium-sized stream and pointed.

"Looks good," Rock whispered as they carefully lowered toward it.

They probably couldn't have gone in undetected in the daylight, but for now Dime stayed to the shadows. She selected a reedy area, away from the structures dotting the stream, hoping to keep them out of sight. Stretching, they rose from the bench and started toward the water.

Rock silently put her hand out, and Dime stopped. At first she wasn't sure how she'd missed the glowstones, but then she saw they'd been lowered into the water, creating a soft light for the small family. Three pyrsi, with the air of parents, hovered around a pair of ch'pyrsi—Dime thought they might be twins—as the young fairies splashed and giggled in the water.

As Dime's own glowstone was in a side pouch, the sturdy canvas kept the light contained. She didn't think the young family could see them, but she supposed they should return to the bench and find another spot. Though it was hard to find a space by water where pyrsi weren't living.

Even the canals, not viewed well by the general burgesses, were populated by the troubled, seeking solace there when they could not, for whatever reasons, elsewhere.

She started to turn back toward the bench. Except Rock had

already lowered to the ground, propping her head into her hands, her elbows on her raised knees, staring out at the gentle current. It was rather like a painting. Dime sat next to her.

Looking across, she realized they were far from alone. A pyr sat on the opposite banks, resting in a reclined chair. Even if xe saw them, there should be no way to see that they were not just fairies, their wings folded behind and maybe a tight cloth over their hair. Not from this distance in the dark.

In the stream, a spray of water was illuminated by the submerged glowstones as the two youths fluttered in the water, their wings stirring the surface. As their children paid no attention, the parents leaned to share, in turn, a soft gentle kiss. One began to sing to the ch'pyrsi, and it was though the night itself were listening to the sweet, if not in-tune, tones of the young parent. It was not a song Dime recognized. Without saying so to Rock, she wondered if her own parent had sung the fairy song to her.

The melancholy of this rang deep, for while she mourned for the pyr or pyrsi's loss with a solemnity that was too pyrsonal to express, she equally felt pangs of weight at the idea of ever being without her father, of a world where they had never met. Without his smile, his fantastical tales, his warmth. She wondered what Gorg would say, sitting here with her, on the banks of a fairy stream, the treetops rustling above them.

Maybe someday they would. He would love it, she knew. Seeing the distant look in Rock's eyes, she wondered whom her friend was thinking of.

Dime wondered what Dayn was doing right now. Subconsciously, her mind materialized the contour of his shoulders and arms. She wished she could pull him close. Or even, just to whisper a few words to him across this big world, share that they were both well. She missed him more than she liked to think about. It hadn't been so long, but it was too long under circumstances such as these.

Luja and Tum—she'd been trying not to dwell on this either. She was glad Rock had made the decision for them: to seek out the newts. Dime knew her children had gone there, to stay with them. The anticipation grew, worry for their well-being. The uncertainty if they were really there, if she'd be with them soon.

She couldn't imagine a world without all of these pyrsi. Da-da. Dayn. Luja. Tum. Ador. Rock. None of whom she would have met in the life she was originally intended to live. And this land, this beautiful fairy land, no longer hers. Her emotions mixed and churned.

Getting to her feet, Dime edged further down the stream, weaving through a line of swaying reeds to avoid being seen. Finding a small clearing, she pushed through to the shore. With silent motions, she rinsed her face and ran a wet cloth under her shirt. Rock, who had followed her, was silent also. They walked back to the bench and Dime took off again, into the darkness.

They went on quite a while until, seeing a distinctive break in the trees, Dime lowered down. "Don't know if you've seen it yet," she said, walking forward to the diamond-dusted net.

"Diamonds in every strand?" Rock ran one hand down a length of rope before drawing it away, like she'd hit a thorn. "Can you imagine how much time this took? How many resources?" She took a step back. "All this time and effort doing *nothing* that helped anyone."

"It's not like we're so perfect," Dime said. "The treatment of the newts is upsetting, once you see it. But were the peckbeaks really less important?" Rock raised an eyebrow. "Ok, what about pyrsi? What about the amount of time spent tattooing a pyr for life just to warn others xe's used some drugs or made a mistake or had bad influences when xe was young? Or even, just did something some high-class pyr didn't like. I'm sure you've been assigned to an outlaw village, right? And just walked around and observed that pyrsi are doing totally normal things and pyrsi's whole careers are assigned to bother them?"

"And meanwhile, we're hiding evidence of the Great War and pretending fairies don't exist." Rock ran her hand over one side of her face. "When will it change? When will our priorities be making lives happier?" She waved a hand. "I know, we change it mind by mind, pyr by pyr. But it gets . . . tiring."

Dime hadn't helped that by showing her the net. "I'm sorry. I'm sorry for stopping." She rubbed her forehead, remembering she had to tell Rock about the newts. Harm, when would this end? "Actually, there's more. The newts were with us when Neimano attacked. Juni carries Tum; they both love it." She thought how to say the next part.

"They did it," Rock muttered, her eyes wide. "Oh, now I get it."

"Yeah. It's different than fairy or soly valence. Purer, in a sense. It like it's made of emotion. The newt, we call her Stern Eyes, reacted to save us—we could *feel* her anger, like it was what struck them directly. Two fairies. Neimano and a guard."

"You call her Stern Eyes? And she likes that? This one, I have to meet. Did it bother her, doing it? Do they have that kind of sense?"

"Yes." Dime had worried about Stern Eyes a lot. She was eager to see her. "They care about each other."

"So Neimano's injury was caused by . . . wow." Rock held her chin. "And he's still not better. What did she do to him? I mean, specifically?"

In all the tension of getting Uchitar out and then the stress of finding Rock, Dime hadn't properly reflected on that. "I actually just saw him again." Rock would know she meant Neimano. "When we found Uchitar. He was weak; he wavered and looked gaunt. But I don't know beyond that. I don't know about his guard, either. Xe struck xyr head, and Tikinal said xe hadn't been back."

"Must be a lot being struck by love when you have no heart."

What? Dime was too tired to think through that, whether newt valence could affect pyrsi differently, or based on their own weaknesses. There was so much they didn't understand.

"Well, let's go." Rock drooped back onto the bench. Neither one of them had slept as the night wore on. She had to stop thinking about it.

It wasn't all noble either, and perhaps part of Rock's encouragement to push on had this in mind. Her children were there, just down that long slope of land. The instinct of a parent drew her with a force greater than sleep.

They rose once more into the sky. Silent again, they flew over the net and out above the remaining trees, not worrying as much now about being seen, not out here where fairy life ceased and newt survival began.

The abruptness of how the trees stopped at the top of the sandy hill had always surprised Dime when Juni took her there, and from above it felt even more so, like the beaches themselves were a border drawn around the land by a careful artist.

A glow emerged ahead: the reflection of the nightlight across the great Sha. Rock reached out, but did not touch her.

"Just a moment? Up here?"

Dime slowed the bench to a halt, letting it hover in place, as they each took a long view of the endless reach of water. "The mountains are pretty too," Dime offered.

"Sure, D. But I've seen them."

Feeling silly for having said it, Dime relaxed into the moment, until they descended again, toward the series of emerging bumps along the shore. Turning to the outside of the line, Dime set the bench into the sand.

It felt like forever since she'd been here. So much had happened since those turns. She couldn't even walk then, on her injured leg, which was now as strong as ever. Feeling uneasy and almost afraid to take her first unaided step onto the loose sand, she teetered just one stride more, in place.

"At least I have clothes, this time."

Rock turned her head. "I do not need *all* your stories."

Dime shrugged, and they walked off toward the beach.

Interlude

"I've never seen anything like it!" Teacher Jana exclaimed as she walked around the small clay sculpture. Her shadow briefly eclipsed the table as she passed the bright lamp and then stopped, setting her heavily tattooed hands on the hips of her striped pants. "You really are extraordinary. I've got to show this to the staff." Turning, she peered in at Gani's face, the way her father inspected produce.

"What's wrong?" her teacher asked.

"I'm fine," Gani answered, keeping her hands wrapped around the base of the figure. She couldn't let Teacher touch the unbaked sculpture, because if she did, she would feel Gani's secret. Teacher would be confused by the warm clay and ask Gani questions that she didn't know how to answer. She glanced at the carving tool on the table. She'd rubbed clay on it, but she'd meant to keep it closer. The brazier was several tables away but at least it was lit.

A rush of sound clattered behind them. Muttering an apology, Teacher Jana left to see what had spilled. With relief, Gani released her hands, looking at the figure posing before her, arm raised, with fabric of a long tunic swirling from one side to the other, tiny fingers pointing to the sky.

It had started without warning, last semester. She'd just come from food prep, and during free time she'd wandered near a sculpture station, noticing it was unattended. It had only been for curiosity that she'd touched the clay; she'd often wondered what it felt like. She'd been sitting with Amme in food prep, and Amme had given her a nice smile. Gani remembered her face warming, but then class had been over.

When she touched the clay, something stirred inside her. Her fingers grew warm, warm like she was ill except, like now, she was fine, and, searching for something to do with them, the shape of Amme flowed through her hands. She'd channeled the unusual heat and the strength of her fingers, and without using any of the carving tools, she pressed and pulled, and when she'd finally taken a breath, Amme stood there in the clay, as glorious as a statue at the Plaza of Sol.

Unable to destroy something so beautiful, she'd tucked it into her cabinet and spent the rest of the session pretending to read in the corner.

She swore she'd never touch clay again.

But her fingers itched. Her mind raced. And when Counselor Lure had walked by the station—she'd tried to show him something simple—he'd talked her parents into signing her up for an advanced art class.

Where, every class, she worried that someone would discover her secret. Would ask how her fingers could grow so hot, how her skin did not burn from the heat. How she found the strength to press clay, bend metal, and form wood without the tools the others used. How the images of beautiful shapes flowed through her fingers as if they'd always been there.

Something was wrong with Gani.

Hiding her hands in her pockets, she murmured an excuse to use the washroom.

Instead, she ran up flight after flight of stairs. So far up, that no one would think to look for her here. Walking around the tower's edge, she snuck outside to the narrow sky garden and crept back against a low wall. Peeking through the springy branches at the skystones, she wondered how long she should stay here. When she'd be ready to face what they might say when she returned.

Part of her wished she could stay in this space between worlds, that a door might open to another one. There, maybe, she could find a life where she could just *be*. Without being as scared to be herself as she was to stop.

She wished she didn't feel so alone.

Act 3

HORIZONS

Juni bounded down the beach, Tum howling a little in her arms. Whatever her child was telling the newt, Dime was pretty sure it included "Slow down!" Tum gasped as Juni sat her into the sand. "She was so excited to see you!" Tum turned to her friend with a scolding, but not angry, look.

SMELL you, Dime thought, but Tum knew how she felt about that, so she appreciated the edit. "Tum, this is my friend, Fe'Rock. Rock, this is Fe'Tum, my child and great friend."

"Hey!" Rock beamed as she sat down next to Tum, which must have taken some concentration since the large newt was towering over them both. "It's so nice to meet you. I've heard you're good at building things. Maybe you can teach me a few tricks?"

"That would be great!" Tum answered with a grin.

Turning to the newt, whose feathers were poofing out in her excitement, Dime wanted to make sure not to make the same mistake this time. "Juni, hello!" Juni reached up and ran her talons through Dime's hair, chattering excitedly. Dime winced as the sharp edges crossed her skin. "Yes, I know. But, look." She pointed to Rock, whose wide-eyed expression held a mix of reactions. "Rock, this is my friend, Juni." She paused. "Tum, please introduce Rock to Juni and also I have an awkwardly belated question. I've always referred to xem with 'she'—is that appropriate?"

"I don't need to ask her that part; she's confirmed before that she's fe'. Their sense of it feels different, but 'she' is appropriate." Tum swung on her arms to face Juni, and clicked and cooed while tilting her head at Rock. Juni turned to Rock excitedly.

Oh, harm. Yet as Dime looked over in trepidation, she was surprised to see Rock not so much as flinch as Juni drew her big ol' tongue across the pyr's face, probably taking off half of the temporary tattoos Rock had drawn on. Rock patted the newt on the arm and raised her brows toward Dime.

"Juni," Dime started, "do you think you could find out if we'll be welcome here? While Tum and I catch up a bit?"

With Tum's translation, Juni straightened up tall, then ran toward the shape of the shelter, down the beach.

Dime embraced her child, settling down next to her and Rock. The way the dry sand shifted against her seat recalled her earlier time here, and Dime subconsciously rested a hand on the arm that had been injured, feeling soft velour and the give of her skin underneath. "First, are you well? Have you been able to eat and drink?" Dime figured they'd brought some food from the Underground, but that would only last so long before they'd have to start foraging from the edge of the forest.

"It's ok for now. Lu's good at finding things and Juni helps ver."

She tried not to think how this qualified her own parenting. "I'm so relieved to see you. I missed you so much. Also—I can't believe you went here on your own!"

Tum did not look remotely chastised, though her face did scrunch with some concern. "I felt a little bad because you and I had just talked about us staying there. Remember, in the shop? And I only meant to be honest. But after you left, Luja and I kept talking, and Da-da was busy back in some tunnels, and the Un . . . place—" Tum's eyes panicked a little at almost saying the Underground's name, so Dime stepped in.

"It's ok. We're all doing our best. What about being flown on a blanket? Was that scary? I have to admit, every time I hear about that, I'm very much 'no, thanks.'"

Tum laughed. Oh, Dime had missed that laugh, somewhere between bubbles and Solshine. "It was fine. The tarps have special ropes, and the fliers kept it very steady. I wasn't scared at all. Or . . . not too much."

"Your chair is at Ador and Batu's home," Dime told her. With that the unspoken fact that Lodon was very far away.

"It's ok for now. I'm doing great." Tum kept glancing behind her. "I'll bet she's sending Lu."

Dime had been glancing also, to see if Luja's form emerged in the dark horizon, but she wanted to learn more about the newts before Juni came back. Tum would have told her if Luja wasn't well.

"Hey. We'll chat soon. But I need to know how things are with the troop. With Stern Eyes. With—" She didn't want to say *the Violence* to someone so young, but Tum seemed to take the meaning.

"Juni helped in keeping Stern Eyes out of trouble, but Stern Eyes mostly mopes now. I was trying to cheer her up, but she didn't want to play games anymore. Then the high newt—we call her *Leader*—arrived with a bunch of other newts and wow, we should probably rename Stern Eyes because Leader has seriously stern eyes. A whole new level. Oh, look, here's Lu."

A familiar figure ran toward them.

Dime stood to meet the outstretched arm of her so-grown child. "Ma-ma," Luja said, not sounding so old in that moment, and Dime pulled ver into a long embrace.

"Luja, this is my friend, Fe'Rock. Rock, this is my child, Ji'Luja." Agni was leaping around Luja's feet. The kita ran over and accepted Dime's silently offered backscratch. Dime had missed Agni's happy rumble against her fingers, and she gave an extra rub behind her ears.

Standing, Rock offered Luja the bridge as if ve were an old colleague. Luja returned it rather rigidly—Rock cast a formidable presence, she remembered—but ve quickly relaxed at Rock's beckoning to sit.

"Luja, it's really my honor. I met your mother a long time ago, and—it's moving to see her child, so—"

Rock was, of course, caught in a bit of an aging dilemma. She'd probably been about to call Luja grown-up or some such thing, then realized that would have the opposite effect on the sensitive Aoch.

"It's really great to meet you," Rock finished instead.

Luja smiled back.

"I dislike rushing this," Dime said, "but I want to figure out the situation before Juni returns. So far, we've gotten that Leader is also stern."

"Harm yeah, she is," Luja said with a slow nod. Dime decided not to comment.

"I'm worried, though." Luja glanced at Tum as if getting her permission to be the one to speak. "It was like the newts were waiting in balance, held by . . . ethics of peace, even when they didn't have peace. Or values of community—maybe that's more how they view it. And they were stretched so far by this. The stride one of the flying two-legs, Sol, I mean the fairies, directly used valence against one of the newts it's like it was a plankbreaker. So if I get it, Leader is basically building up a huge group of newts that will all march to Home Sha together. They don't want any harm—"

She met Rock's eyes. It was clear neither of them could imagine a scenario where hundreds of newts march into the new, high-class fairy village and the Violence wasn't breached.

"What does Leader think of you?" Dime asked, as Agni rolled up against Rock's leg.

"Da-da was right," Luja answered, with Tum nodding beside ver. "They view us as cubs. So their instinct is only to care for us, not even to interact with us as neighbors."

Dime imagined Luja did not enjoy admitting that, so she moved on. "What do you think about Rock and me approaching Leader?"

Luja turned vis head. "I think it's about to be moot because Juni went and told all the elders anyway. And she's almost back."

Craning in the dark, Dime did not yet hear or see Juni. Yet it wasn't long until she did, the newt's light-colored feathers reflective in the nightlight. Without her usual energy, Juni seemed subdued, as she'd been when she returned Tum to the old woods. The newt grunted and muttered, her back slumped.

"We're supposed to go to the common area now," Tum said, her solemn tone matching Juni's affect.

"Is something wrong?"

"No, I don't think so," Tum answered. "Nothing new, I mean. They said something Juni didn't like, but either I'm not understanding what or she doesn't want to talk about it."

Looking directly at Juni, Dime could see her eyes held a touch of a plea. She decided not to press. "Ready for this?" she said to Rock.

"Sure am." Rock was clearly trying not to stare at Juni. She could understand; the newts were uniquely beautiful when one first saw them up close. Wait until she saw them in the light.

As Juni lifted Tum and Agni ran on ahead, Rock walked closer to Dime, the faint scent of a candy mint wafting from her. "How is it," she asked, "that your entire family is so amazing?"

Rather than acknowledge Rock's gibe, she simply answered her. "I wonder that a great deal myself. They are all pretty excellent; I admit it." And she was thinking of Dayn as they walked up to the common area. Was he still in the Underground? Would he come here? Dime had no way to know.

The common area had changed tremendously: the rocky overhang was still in place, but instead of a loose shield of spindly branches to lessen the wind, a tightly woven wall surrounded the space, with doorways positioned not to allow the rain or breezes into the center. A strip of ceiling had been left open on the beach side, which would allow some light in during the daytime, and even now, kept the space from the prevalent feeling of darkness. While the sides were still lined with mud seats, some wooden structure had been added: trunks or chunky benches for seats. The design of it all was so familiar.

Then she remembered that Dayn had stayed here a short while, and had worked on its construction. Juni rubbed Dime's arm and pointed, grunting under her breath.

"She says that Da-da has a name. Like . . . a newt name."

Even Dime knew by now that was a huge deal. She rubbed Juni's arm in return, taking care not to bend the feathers back. "Can I hear it?" Dime thought, especially with Juni, any presumption on that would slide.

And when Juni spoke Dayn's name, just a short series of sounds that ended just as soon as it began, she had to fight back the tears in her eyes.

"Do you think I have a name?" she asked Tum.

As if surmising the question, Juni scrunched her face.

"You can't ask that," Tum whispered. "It's super rude. Names are always given."

"Sorry," Dime muttered, glad she was at least in a forgiving crowd.

"They like you, Ma-ma. Isn't that nice enough?"

"It is," she whispered, quieting as they walked to the center of the shelter, her bag left leaning against Rock's, outside. She didn't recognize anyone that fit the description of Leader, not the way her children had reacted to the elder newt. Dime suspected this Leader was aware of their presence, though, so moving to an area unoccupied by any newts, she sat down into the sand. She glanced around. At least three dozen newts were there, maybe four, within the space, and through the doorways she could see many others milling around on the beach. Inside the shelter, some of the newts were raised onto seats, and some sat on what looked like grass mats, the type Tum was good at weaving.

Those resting there peered at her suspiciously. Dime had the sense most would have greeted her, but with Leader in the camp, they were deferring to see her reaction first. Still, Dime smiled around at them, and a few grunted or scratched their sides.

Rock sat next to her, mostly quiet except for whispering "wow" in her ear. At least Rock had been warned and had an idea what to expect. Dime had arrived here in a thong, unable to walk, and with a clay cast on her arm.

Speaking of which, to the back of the larger seats, she noticed something new. A sculpture, she thought, made of a packed clay. Its shape was roughly like a pyr, but with the broader shoulder shape and hunch of a newt. She had to imagine a little to see it as a figure, but the shape was there. "Tum, this sculpture? Does it serve a purpose?"

"Yes. It's art," Tum answered, not bothering to lower her voice. "Large Hands made it. He loves to sculpt."

Hearing a grunt behind them, Dime turned to see a newt with somewhat ragged feathers rising up on his hind legs, swinging his backside around. As he sat again, he held up his taloned hands, boasting them to Dime.

"Oh, yes," she said, "very impressive!" The newt beamed back. Glancing around, Dime noticed something else. The newts weren't really looking at her. They were looking at Rock.

When Juni had first brought her to the troop, they'd had some animal sense that she was a fairy by blood. A generosity on their part that Dime had not grasped until much later.

So they must know Rock was a soly. It's not that they were unfamiliar with solies; Ella had been their longest pyr friend. And her children were here. Yet, they stared, without any shame, at Rock with pure curiosity. She was new, Dime supposed. They'd seen Dime before.

Rock did not answer them or acknowledge the stares. Ah, Rock was waiting for Leader too. And here Dime probably looked like the crude one, grinning and asking about Large Hands' sculpture. Was that really the best name they could do? That said, he'd been real proud of those hands. So if Tum called him that, it's probably because it's what he wanted.

The newts became silent and their fidgeting ceased. Juni scooted back into a shadow. An old-looking newt entered the shelter, walking mostly with the aid of her hands against the ground. Dime realized she had no idea the life span of a newt or how it compared to a pyr. Yet there wasn't a way this newt hadn't lived for many cycles, or even into epochs, because it would take that long to form the smooth chips on her scales and the lines in her face. It was hard to tell the color of her thinning feathers in the dark, but they looked brownish, with many fading to a peach on the tips.

Before Dime could decide whether or how to approach her, she caught another familiar face. Stern Eyes, following behind her, with a whole different stance than when Dime had first met this troop's leader. Wanting to make her allegiance clear, Dime stepped forward and bowed deeply to Stern Eyes. Then, hoping it would balance, she turned and bowed—just a tiny bit deeper—to Leader.

Leader sat back on her legs, chewing on a stick.

Tum walked forward, settling right next to Dime. Grateful, Dime reached down to give Tum's upper arm a little squeeze. Seeing that Leader was going to remain seated, Dime sat as well. She leaned in toward Tum.

"If I say something awful, you don't have to translate it exactly," Dime said.

"I know," Tum answered. Their eyes met, and in that closeness and comfort, Dime felt a new spark of energy. She turned back to Leader.

"I am sorry for what pyrsi have done to you."

Tum's translation was short.

"I know that you are considering traveling to Home Sha." This invoked a loud series of screeches from around the shelter, but Dime wanted to make sure she could continue. "I ask you to wait just a while longer."

Tum continued to translate, though she seemed to be struggling to get the ideas across.

"Not to wait because you should wait, but because I am worried about anyone getting hurt."

"We are hurt," Tum translated. "We are sick on these short time beds. Sorry, I think that means like temporary."

"I am sorry you are sick. And I know it is hard here."

Leader spoke slowly and pushed her hands together. Dime was used to Juni's pronounced emotions, and she wasn't as sure how to read Leader. If she could guess, through the newt's wrinkled face, her eyes were sad. As she spoke, other newts started to murmur in response, but hushed as Leader's arm hit her chest.

Tum looked over at Dime nervously. "She says it's not just a hurt because they are sick. It is a hurt because Home Sha is their home. Even if they were not sick, they should be able to live at home."

Dime thought about that. "I'm sorry. I had to leave my home, too. I should have understood better."

The next part Dime didn't really need translated. Leader's wide eyes said it all.

"What do you want?" Tum asked.

"I don't want to fix this hurt with more hurt," Dime said. "I want to work together to make"—she almost said pyrsi—"us happy. I am asking for two things." She paused for Tum to explain. "The first thing is that I have learned there is something dangerous deep in the diamond caves. Something that could make pyrsi sick. I am scared and I want to go . . . destroy it. To do that, I would ask for your advice on how to get into the diamond caves without the Seats knowing."

Tum seemed to struggle with *Seats*, and Dime said, "Tell her the leaders of the flying two-legs." That seemed to work.

"Second, I would ask you not to go to Home Sha quite yet. Let me destroy the dangerous thing and then let me try again to get the leaders to talk. Both of them: the fairy and soly."

Dime wasn't surprised to see the annoyance on the newt's face. She knew the newts had no trust in any pyr right now.

"For this thing," Tum began, "I will not tell you what I will do. I will think about your thoughts. Advice, maybe that means advice. I will trust you that there is a bad thing in Sha's heart. But this is also hard." While Tum had been talking, Dime had missed some sort of side conversation, and now Stern Eyes moved forward.

Instead of her usual speech, Stern Eyes began rumbling and pushing against the ground. Dime looked to Tum in confusion.

"It's the Boring Project, Ma-ma."

WHAT? Now this? She hadn't felt the drilling; Dime hoped maybe Sala had stopped it. "Is she saying they are drilling again?"

The newts glanced around at each other, and Dime understood: they could feel it right now. "Tell them we can't feel it."

Tum did, and several newts peered over at Dime as if being kind about her inferior body. "So," she said, not liking the feel of their eyes and judgment, "is it over the caves? The boring? Close to the diamonds?"

Stern Eyes indicated that it was.

Now this too? Dime wondered how this would impact finding Neimano's room. They had to find it before he was able to act or before the Circles crushed the whole place.

"Neimano is the fairy who hurt us," Dime said. "Who hurt Juni and Stern Eyes." The newts looked uncomfortable, and Stern Eyes stared at the floor. "He has made a . . . netting out of valence around the diamond caves. If we go in the fairy way, he will know. I want to get inside without him knowing. At least until the very end, when there may be no choice."

When Tum had finished, Stern Eyes reached politely for the stick Leader had been chewing, and with a shrug, she handed it over. With a slow stream of clicks and grunts, Stern Eyes carved a series of lines and circles on the ground. Perhaps it was a map, but the lines overlapped and sometimes didn't connect at all and Dime couldn't understand it. Tum's expression showed she didn't either. Dime glanced back at Rock, thinking it might be a Fo-ror code, but Rock shook her head.

Tum quietly told Stern Eyes something, perhaps that they didn't know the symbols. Frustrated, Stern Eyes sat back and grumbled.

"She doesn't see how we can't understand," Tum said. "Even

though they talk to each other, and my way of doing it is really rough, I don't think they think of it as language. So those symbols are how you tell other newts where things are. You don't learn that. You just know it, she seems to be saying. She also says the newts are sad for Ada-ji. They can feel all the cracks that the two-legs are making. The smaller passages are broken. Only the ones along the Heartline work anymore."

"The Heartline?"

"I'm not . . . exactly sure," Tum said. "But it felt like a heart and a line. Maybe I got it wrong. Anyway, they know a way to get in. Stern Eyes is embarrassed you cannot understand tunnels and she will have to take—" Tum laughed. "She switched it to the two-arms. I think she's worried about me, since they keep saying two-legs."

Tum made a series of sounds. "I told her it was fine. I said I don't need legs. And somewhere out there, someone probably has no arms."

Stern Eyes looked troubled, and Tum thought a moment before speaking in newt. The newt brightened back up.

"I made up a new sound. Said it means all the pyrsi who are not newts. She liked that and said she would say it instead of two-legs. She says she will need to go with us."

Dime was thinking about the newt accompanying them. She wasn't sure that would work. "I feel uncomfortable putting her at risk. Besides," Dime glanced over to where the light-feathered newt sat, scratching her hip. "If Stern Eyes goes, you know our friend will want to go too. Unless Leader says no."

Stern Eyes jumped up and her sounds were percussive, like she was angry. These newts always seemed to understand her at the most inconvenient times.

"If there is a bad thing from the bad pyr," Tum followed her, "then we will help you find it. You do not choose where we go."

Juni lumbered over to Stern Eyes' side, folding her scaled arms over each other.

"Ok, let me ask you this." Dime knew she was shifting the

subject, but she was still considering how to address the last piece. Besides, she'd feel better with a second opinion. "Is it appropriate to destroy the bad thing, if it isn't mine?"

"Is it bad?" Tum repeated Leader's question back.

Their mouths opened with a bit of a squeal and then held open just a while, and Dime realized the newts were laughing at her again. One complete stranger walked over and pet her, like she was cute. Alright. That was enough of this.

She thought again about the whole situation. It had been complicated enough already: to see if she can get the governments together and negotiate a way forward. And she'd wound her way past detour after detour but was still determined to get there. Then it had become more complicated: Neimano had a way to kill a whole lot of pyrsi and perhaps restart the Great War. So she had to take care of that first. Now, it was more complicated. The Ja-lal, for whatever reason, were boring again, which was also likely to restart the Great War.

How could she move toward peace while at the same time just preventing everyone from destroying it?

The Ja-lal were probably at the most risk from Neimano's scheme. Used to generally good health, the impact of a severe disease could harm scores of Ja-lal before they figured out what was going on. And the Fo-ror were at the most risk from whatever the Circles were doing. The boring had concerned Dime before, and Dayn's analysis had only made her more worried. If the structure of the rocks collapsed, it could be as devastating as the curse, both from the physical damage it could cause, but especially if it cut off the water flow to Pito.

On top of all this, just going into the caves—especially with newts—could be seen as an attack by the Fo-ror and could provoke the same conflict she was trying to prevent. It could give Neimano fuel. Maybe she wasn't thinking right, and she should just approach the other Seats directly. But Tikinal had said not to. Agent X had said not to. What would they do that they hadn't already done? This group was probably the best equipped to actually do something without alerting Neimano.

Leader's gruff sounds pulled her back to the moment.

"She says you think a lot for a pyr," Tum said. "She's using the word I made up." Tum grinned.

Rock chuckled beside her. "She's super musey."

Out of nowhere, it felt like, Luja walked forward to stand in front of Leader. "If Juni and Stern Eyes will go, then I will go also." She turned to Dime. "I'm a medic, Ma-ma. You may need one. Please. Let me go."

Leader started to react. Dime opened her mouth.

Tum turned back and forth, with a confused look on her face. "Everyone, you have to talk one at a time so I can help." She moved her hand at Leader with a string of sounds.

Leader bowed slightly to Tum before jumping right back into speaking. Communicating, really, as the language seemed as much about the gestures.

"Leader isn't sure about Stern Eyes and Juni going," Tum said. "Their bravery leads to a better name, but she worries whether they would encounter bad pyrsi, and if they are so brave, she may need them here."

Dime held her tongue. The first reaction was that Juni and Stern Eyes should be allowed to go wherever they want. Containing a pyr was the Violence. Then she thought about all the ways her eyes had been opened to the restrictive policies of both Ja-lal and Fo-ror. Hemsa, arrest, class restrictions. Harm, she'd been thinking how to tell Luja ve couldn't go either. Dime sighed. Maybe pyrsi could get their own ethics in a row before they lectured someone else.

Juni walked forward, whimpering, her body pulled low as though pleading with Leader. Tum stayed quiet, but Dime saw the gist of it. Juni said she was her own newt and asked if she could go, and Leader said she was a cub and she would do what Leader said.

Dime did not expect Stern Eyes to step forward and join in.

Tum kept trying to catch her eye. Dime leaned over so Tum could speak into her ear.

"Stern Eyes is making the case that the bad thing could maybe hurt the newts too. That it's in their best interest to go. But I actually think she's trying to protect Juni from getting in trouble."

Sol. Dime hadn't even considered whether the newts could catch this disease. That was reason for them not to go.

Tum's urgency increased. "They've put Leader in a tough spot. She could lessen both of their names, but just the idea of this troop's leader defying her right now would weaken her ability for everyone else to see her fully in charge. Especially with both of them arguing. It's like . . . there's too many others watching. It's too distracting with us here. It's like she's holding back, and the other newts are sensing that too. I don't like how this feels."

Dime had to decide if it was worth causing even more of a stir, but if Tum felt things were going a bad way, she trusted her. Time to take a chance. She rose and stepped forward, toward Leader, glancing at the statue behind her, like maybe it could help. She took a shaky breath. "Leader, I know that the newts have valence of feelings." As Tum hesitantly repeated this from behind her, several newts moved forward from the edges of the space, closing in on the center. Leader screamed, and Dime could feel an emotion in the air: *Fear.*

The line between emotion and valence seemed thin for the newts; Dime suddenly understood that better. They had controlled it through strict command, a command that hung on Leader's signal. Dime may have just made a critical mistake. Would Leader use it here? How precious was this secret?

"Wait," Dime said. She lowered to the floor, crawling to meet the elder newt. Reaching into her pocket, she took out the little carving. The good luck charm Rock had made her on the ledge of the cliff. A pang of sadness hit her, but she couldn't think what else to offer with her bag sitting outside. Not her dice. And she still had the owl. She wished she could glance to Rock, to say she was sorry, but there wasn't time.

She reached forward with the charm, and curious, Leader lifted it, sniffing the carved wood as she turned it around.

Dime hurried to speak. "I know because I was there. And I want you to know what Stern Eyes did." She pointed at Stern Eyes, who looked entirely frozen, as Tum scrambled to translate. "She protected the cubs. Juni and Tum were with us." Dime pointed at them both.

"The bad pyr used his valence to hold us in place. We were scared, so scared Stern Eyes could feel it. And when Juni was scared too, Stern Eyes jumped ahead. We saw the pyrsi afterward. They were both able to leave. Stern Eyes made a quick choice, and she chose to protect us. I don't know if that's right or wrong but surely it's forgivable." Dime rose to a low seat. "I do not want them to be in danger either, but I could use her bravery on my quest to destroy the bad thing. If you would assign her to go, and Juni too, because she would be too worried about us if she stayed here, I would think that very wise."

Leader waited for Tum to conclude, then she responded in short clicks, waving the air in front of her.

"She wants us to leave," Tum said. "Not leave the Beds. Just out of her sight. Until she can think."

"Let's go," Dime said, and they walked outside, Dime and Rock picking up their bags. The sand spread before them, sloping downward to the broad waters of Sha, and Dime could make out the bumps of the newts' burrows spaced along the beach. They moved more slowly without Tum's chair or without Juni to carry her, but Dime thought the newts would understand. They all seemed to adore Tum; they must be used to how she moved.

Dime had a feeling Juni wasn't supposed to follow them, but she did. No licking or hugs—the newt ambled a good distance behind, her arms drooping low. They stopped for her to catch up.

"Sorry about giving away the carving," Dime said.

"D. If that carving kept us from getting sparked back there, I'll make you a new one." Rock was almost laughing.

"I kept the owl," Dime said.

"I know." She smiled.

"Tum, are you ok? I don't like you having to be in the middle like this." *You're just a ch'pyr,* she didn't add.

As polite as Tum was, her return expression was quite sarcastic. Dime decided to stop worrying about it for now. With Juni dragging along, it seemed her efforts were better placed there. "What about you, Juni? Are you alright? I'm sorry that you are facing all this conflict—" She almost finished with *because of me,* but the last time she'd said something along those lines, the newts hadn't reacted well. They didn't seem to think this was about Dime at all, which was a pretty refreshing change, actually.

Now they were all stopped, and Dime noticed Tum hadn't translated her last query to Juni. Rock had one hand on her hip and was gazing off, the way she did when unsure. Luja looked deep in thought. Dime was feeling a little lost, herself. It was Tum who spoke. Or, whatever it should be called when she made the newt noises and gestures. In response, Juni perked up, grabbed Tum, and ran off in the direction of what Dime knew was Juni's burrow. Tum tried to call something back, but Dime couldn't make it out.

Luja laughed. "Sometimes Juni doesn't wait. She also forgets how fast she is compared to me. I think we're going that way."

Soon, they reached Juni's burrow, dug into the sandy beach. Even in the daylight, only the front area of each burrow was illuminated. But, like when Dime had arrived here, in the nightlight the burrows were completely dark inside. Even more so to those with soly vision. Figuring Tum was inside, she called in, "Can I turn on a glowstone, or will that bother her?"

She had no idea what customs might apply or whether the use of fairy valence was offensive. But even Dime knew Juni well enough to discern her response was one of delight, before Tum had even translated it.

Dime recharged the stone she'd grabbed in the forest, though not brightly. Holding it out, she ducked through the entrance. Inside and standing to full height, she saw Juni's burrow in a way she never had before. The collection around the arched doorway seemed to have grown substantially now that she had some access beyond the net. Dime wouldn't have mentioned it, but she'd clearly been making extra trips into the forest.

The little polished stones and glass fragments had been pretty in the filtered daylight, but here in the directed light of the glowstone, they sparkled like jewels. Dried sprigs of all types, many holding delicate little wildflowers, were pressed into the mud like a suspended garden, accented by the colors of little scraps of fabric. And in the middle, the tiny jade lizard was not just well-placed, it was now framed, surrounded by perfectly matched little blue stones, and mud smoothed down like enamel, as though set by a jeweler.

"Tum, let me say this to her, please." Dime turned to face Juni and swept her hand out over the entrance display. "This is beautiful art." Then she placed that hand over her chest.

Normally, Juni might leap or touch her if she liked what Dime did or said. But here, Juni just stood in place, the light of the glowstone reflecting her wide lavender eyes. Dime could feel her joy.

She understood. This was art. When the turns felt wrong, friends suffered, and leaders disappointed—there was always art. And there was never a time not to stop and appreciate each small instance of beauty, joy, and soul.

Dime thought back to the ladle in Nafat's museum. Here, a high-class pyr of immense wealth had spent his life curating objects of value for others, but when he had the chance to make his own place, he had chosen to center a spoon.

Art was not wealth or rarity, or sometimes even skill.

Art was life.

Juni sat down against the curved burrow wall and murmured to Tum.

"She says if we need a rest, we can stay here and sleep."

The idea was tempting, and Dime could see that in Rock's eyes as well. They'd been up a long time now. And Dime had slept here before, and it wasn't terrible. But not now, not yet.

With a nod from Juni, Dime walked to the back room of the

burrow, curious, as she'd never seen it in the light. She stepped downward, into the section dug deeper into the sand and the clay below it. Rock and Luja filed past, and only Tum stayed in the front with Juni. Dime was amused to see that Agni was curled up at the back of the sleeping area, her front leg over her face.

"Fascinating," Rock whispered. "Have you ever seen a room before that was not designed to be seen?"

Dime wasn't sure she had. Luja drew in a slow breath. "That's so interesting. Look, Ma-ma, nothing here provides a visual, but it is all beautiful to touch and feel. The padding of the sleeping area. The rounding of the wall, shaped just to Juni's back."

"Even the acoustics," Rock added. "Stop, listen a stride." They grew silent. "Listen to the way the sound mutes and shapes. I can barely hear Tum and Juni, out there, yet the rhythm of the water against the beach creates a low percussion, like a heartbeat."

"I always slept in the common area," Luja said. "Three felt like too many in here." She glanced at Agni. "Four. I think they thought it was rude, but they put up with it."

Dime felt amused imagining the elder newts rolling their eyes at the Aoch sleeping in their commons the way a pyr would side-eye one sprawled across the couch.

They walked back into the front area, and again, she complimented the burrow, a concept that Juni seemed to understand just fine.

"Juni?" It was Rock's voice behind her. Dime watched as she, with a quick jerking motion of both hands, snapped a button from the top of her shirt. It was a deep blue button, probably resin that had been poured into a little brass ring. She held it out.

Dime hadn't explained the significance of gifts here, but Rock had seen Leader's reaction to the carving. With a squeal, Juni lifted Rock into the air and spun her, almost knocking Dime and Luja over in the small burrow as Tum scooted to one side, laughing. Rock just laughed, looking not even slightly disturbed that she was being tossed about by an animal.

This was enough burrow for Dime. "I'll be outside," she said, walking back out into the night. It wasn't long before the others joined her, Juni included.

"Can we go to the beach?" Rock was asking and who knew what was being understood or translated anymore; Dime just yawned as she followed the group down closer to the water's edge. The air had a strong odor as they drew near, reminding her with a jolt of the time she'd tried to drink the Sha water. As a scent, it was musky but not unpleasant. She took a deep breath.

No one objected as Dime made sure to position herself in between her children as they sat in a line facing the rippling, dark Sha. When she'd arrived here, the joy of seeing her children again—and seeing them safe and happy—had been tempered by the idea that again, *again*, she'd have to leave them in order to find Neimano's cave. But Luja had offered to go with them, and could she really turn down the assistance from one she'd seen time and time again to be remarkably capable? Yet were five—herself, Luja, Rock, Stern Eyes, and Juni—too many for a covert mission? She knew they were, but who would she ask to stay behind?

She was not willing for Tum to go. Tum was capable also, but she was young, and her mobility required extra attention. This was accommodated in a tower or city, but in a dangerous cave as the drills rumbled overhead? Either way, this was too much for a ch'pyr. She hoped Tum would understand. Except—she wouldn't leave Tum here alone, not without Juni. Maybe she could stay with Volana, just until they got back from the caves? Volana could probably get word to Dayn.

And those harmed-off drills. Had Sala not trusted her? Forget trusting her; had she not even bothered to check? She tried to remind herself not a great amount of time had really passed. No time at all, by the standards of the Circles.

Luja reached a hand out over the coarse ground, and Dime placed hers over it, grateful for the small gesture.

Again, she returned to the thought she'd had earlier, by the stream. What would her life be like without the pyrsi that now filled its core?

She knew there would be another life. Other pyrsi. But she didn't want to imagine that life, not after having lived this one. Whatever had been done to her. Whatever missteps she'd made. They were hers, as Ador had said. He was right. She felt that now.

"I'd never seen Sha before," Rock said. "I'm having a hard time believing it's real."

She wasn't used to hearing Rock speak abstractly, but if anything could awe a pyr, it would be the vast expanse of water.

"You can really float," Tum said, her voice increasing in pitch. "Da-da and Luja and Agni and I floated on a mat that we made."

"I think it's called a raft," Dime said. Someone at the Underground had told her that.

"It is," Tum agreed. "I only got to go once, but Da-da and Luja went twice."

"I flew a glider once," Rock said. "It was one of the best things I've ever done."

"Oh?" Luja turned with interest.

"Yeah. This company would take you up into the foothills, and you'd strap on to this big kite, basically, then they'd knock you off and you'd float down into a field."

"Harm." That sounded awful. "Who would do that?"

"I'm sorry; you flew all over Ada-ji in a rickety chair?"

"Sure, but I was in control of that. You basically just jumped off a mountain."

"Ma-ma, that makes it sound amazing," Luja interjected.

Rock laughed. "Yes! See. If you want, I can take you sometime. It's exhilarating."

Dime clamped her mouth shut. This was only getting worse. "Is Juni alright?"

The newt was sitting back, not atop her limbs as she often did.

"She's fine. She sometimes needs a stride," Tum answered. "Ga-da says creatures live in the Sha."

In fairness, her father had a whole tale about a twelve-legged jelly monarch who collected lost dreams. But she didn't think Tum meant that. "I suppose they could. Animals live in the lakes and streams, after all." Pyrsi from Lodon never spent much time around unfiltered water, so the idea of water-life was always particularly foreign. Still, she'd seen it in a few of the Nor Lodon estates, with small ponds that were built off of mountain streams.

"I wonder if there are cities in the water," Tum mused. "Maybe if some pyrsi can fly in the air, others can live in the Sha."

"Now that sounds like a fun story to write," Dime said. "One of these days, maybe you and Ga-da can write some lyrics, and I'll put them to a song."

No one had a response for that, and Dime leaned back against her arms. She was glad no one was asking about Neimano's cave. Having a break from thinking about it was restful. Even a short break. Except she was thinking about it. *Ugh.*

"Maybe the water pyrsi are just like us," Luja said, now joining in on the water pyrsi business. "Except with big fins. Maybe there's a Tum down there, imagining air pyrsi." Ve chuckled, less serious than before. "I like thinking about this. Tum, maybe you'll be a writer."

"I like building things," Tum said. "Like Uchitar. I'd like to be like him."

Rock sighed. Dime knew she'd grown fond of the tall fairy in the short time she'd known him, and Dime had told her how they'd found him in the prison. She was probably worried.

"Tum, did you know that your mother and I saw ch'pyrsi playing inside the water? Like a bathing tub, but splashing around together."

"What about the animals? Were they in there with them?"

"You're in the air right now with animals," Luja answered. Arching back, Dime could see a few birds gliding silently overhead.

"Ok, what about their clothes? Wouldn't they get wet?"

"Our clothes get wet if it rains," Luja answered. "Maybe it's like that."

"I'm gonna go in it." Rock shimmied her bag off, unclipped

about a dozen pouches, and then rose, as Dime sat there, trying to figure out if she was for real.

"Wait!"

Rock had already run off toward the water. Juni was already ahead of her. Dime sighed, waving on her children. "Fine." She hoped this was safe. The water had nearly choked her when she'd tried to drink it. Would it hurt them? Maybe they should be more careful? Who was the grown-up here, anyway?

She'd touched the water before. It hadn't hurt her or left any marks; she just couldn't drink it. They all seemed fine as they waded in, joking with each other amidst Tum's excited squeals. Yet Dime couldn't quite bring herself to join them. There was just too much on her mind. Stretching her legs, she watched with curiosity as they bounced around in the water. She wasn't sure whether Rock or Juni was keeping a closer eye on Tum, but Luja didn't leave her side either. From the exuberant splashes, they seemed to be having fun.

After not too long, they all came giggling up the beach, Luja and Rock running circles around each other in clingy wet clothes, and Juni shaking water from her feathers, spraying the rest of the group with more of the pungent water. Dime craned to see Tum's shape in the darkness, and was glad to see that Juni had run back to meet her, patiently waiting as Tum made her way up.

"Ah, I've got grainy stuff all over me," Rock complained, shaking herself off almost as Juni had. "I'd use my blanket to dry off, but then it would get grainy too."

"We all make our own beds," Dime muttered.

"Not true," Rock argued. "Don't you have any high-class friends? They hire pyrsi to clean their homes, and they never even have to wash the sheets." Luja chuckled to her side.

Dime grimaced. "Make your bed doesn't mean make your bed. It means select your bed. Make your choices. Wait, why am I telling you this? You know everything. My goodness, you smell like gullyweed." This was only getting more annoying.

"So, high-class pyrsi can get designers too. They pick everything, from beds to coordinating lamps. They'll even build the furniture to match the shape of the room. They—"

"I was being metaphorical," Dime grumbled.

"D. Clue in. So was I."

"Ma-ma, stop." Luja was holding vis sides. "You're always just doing what she wants."

At least that got Rock to change the subject. "Tum, do you need anything?"

"No. But that was so fun!"

Dime forgot about whatever else had been going on as Tum drew near and Dime saw the size of the smile on her face, the excitement in her eyes. Her heart aching, she considered that while Tum kept to good spirits, she hadn't had much chance to be carefree. To play with other youth. Even in the Underground, her play had been in a full-up maker room, filled with pyrsi many times her age.

"I'm glad you had fun," Dime said, trying not to watch Juni as she licked the sand off her own toes.

"Next time, maybe you can go."

So many emotions rose, Dime couldn't even explain them to herself. "Sure," she stammered out. "Maybe you're right." Going now wouldn't do anything. Still, she stared down at the rippling Sha, just missing the peace of a turn with her family—the whole family— without having to worry. Just for a while.

They couldn't wait much longer. She was tired, they needed to get to the diamond caves, and the others would undoubtedly start itching soon from whatever was coating their skin.

"Do you think solies used to live here?" Tum was leaning on one arm, rubbing it with the other.

"What?" Dime thought she had heard her, but wanted to be sure.

Rock and Luja drew closer.

"Do you think before the Great War, solies and fairies lived all over Ada-ji?"

"I think they did," Rock answered.

Dime looked at her in surprise.

"The Seats' complex. Why isn't it in the trees?"

"Because it's attached to the diamond caves."

"Yes, I'm aware." Rock made a face. "But the design of it seems meant to accommodate solies."

"Maybe it used to be the solies' complex," Luja contemplated aloud. "Maybe that's what started the Great War."

"I don't think so," Rock said. "It's also built for wings. The size of the corridors and the ledges along the large domed ceilings in some of the larger areas suggest it was also built for fairies."

"It makes me mad," Luja said. "We should know all this stuff. And I just don't believe there's no record, that no one wrote anything down. So obviously the Circles hid it all—or destroyed it—what didn't they want us to know?"

"That's the worst part about what they've done," Rock replied. "At some point when the events are hidden, pyrsi forget what it even was that they've hidden."

"It makes me mad," Luja repeated.

"Sometime you should talk to Ella," Dime said, cautiously. She wasn't going to reveal what Ella said about locating pre-War texts and hiding them in her home, but maybe Ella would share those, if someone cared. "She's a journalist; I think she's learned quite a bit over the cycles. You could ask her."

By Luja's silence and hard-set eyes, Dime felt certain ve would do that.

Distracted by motion, Dime turned to see Stern Eyes running toward them. She didn't seem to notice the wet clothes, but spoke directly to Juni and Tum, together. At first, she grunted confidently, like it was a message. Then, she scratched behind her ear and sat down. Dime sensed there was some conflict in what she'd said. Nervously, she glanced over at Dime, then away.

"Ma-ma, I'm not totally sure because their whole way of thinking it is different, but I think Stern Eyes is saying thank you. Thank you for standing up for her back there."

"Oh. No. That was nothing." Dime would always help her friend;

she'd been scared she'd gone too far! Remembering how the newts reacted to touch, Dime approached her with outstretched arms. In contrast to Juni's exuberant reactions, Dime was surprised with the gentleness of how Stern Eyes pulled Dime into her grasp.

Her feathers were more rigid than Juni's, and without much of the soft underlayer. Her scales felt rough against Dime's fingers. Yet Dime had rarely felt such comfort as she did, held in this quiet, long embrace. Knowing Stern Eyes must feel very upset, she did not let go, waiting until the newt's arms finally released.

Dime breathed in, trying not to let emotion overwhelm her. Something in the older newt's pain had opened a small window into her own.

"We're supposed to go to Leader now," Tum said, as she reached up for Juni to lift her. Everyone was quiet—not just quiet but bearing a quiet energy—as they walked back to the common area.

"Hey, can you at least dry us off?" Rock asked, mock irritation in her voice.

Dry you off? Oh. Dime swept a small amount of valence into a wind toward Rock, and Luja and Juni, Tum in her arms, joined her. Juni made a series of high-pitched noises but stayed in place as Tum stretched out one arm, then the other. Luja and Rock each turned to face away, and Dime didn't appreciate that Rock bent over, letting out a sing-song *whoo* noise. A spray of sand and mist flew off of them, including one of Juni's feathers. Juni didn't seem concerned.

"That's way better," Rock said with a sigh, as they started off again. "Still, I won't turn down a shower." She glanced up. "Not sure if they have sudden rainstorms, but I'd take one of those too. Anyone want a mint?" The newts didn't like the smell of the colorful squares, but Luja and Rock happily enjoyed theirs as they walked toward the shelter.

This time, Leader had climbed onto a sanded tree stump—Dayn must have made that, she thought with fondness—so she was elevated over the other newts. Fewer were here than before—maybe only twenty now—and those who remained all looked older as well. Except for Juni, who seemed glued into Stern Eyes' shadow. A few of the newts sniffed, and Juni murmured something low.

Dime slowly removed the still-lit glowstone from her pocket, and with no one objecting, the soft light illuminated the participants.

Leader pretended not to notice. She waited for them to all sit, and then she tapped a stick against the side of the stump and spoke.

"She says we are permitted to go. Stern Eyes and Juni—Ma-ma, she called Juni 'the cub'—are ordered to accompany us and ensure the bad thing is destroyed." Tum fumbled a little over the word *destroyed*, as it was usually a word reserved for terrible disasters, not plans. Again, Dime felt sad that Tum had to be part of this world, where such things were discussed, but for now that world was real, and she would not hide her from it.

Leader's communication grew agitated.

"There is not much time. She is not going to wait and see her cubs attacked by pyrsi, or watch the last of the tunnels smash, or watch one more friend be sick of eating or of love." Tum paused. "I'm not sure I got all that right." With Leader continuing, Tum rushed to catch up. "Watching Home Sha be changed without us *is* the Violence. Letting us hurt is the Violence. They have placed us— I'm not sure what she is saying."

Dime knew. "They have placed us in a situation where we can't win. Where we must make heart-wrenching choices."

Rock gazed over with a rather sad smile, meant, she knew, to be encouraging.

"Each troop will gather here," Tum continued. "They will build the . . . force of Sha. I will not wait long. I will not wait for you or for anyone. I have my choices. Or, maybe I make my decisions. I can make my decisions."

"It's ok, we understand," Dime said.

"The safest way is the water. Or . . . the end of water. I think that's how she's saying it."

This was sounding entirely too ominous for Dime.

Tum turned to Juni and asked her something in newt. Juni tittered but not unkindly—more like Tum wasn't saying something right.

Juni ran to the side of the shelter and scooped a handful of sand. It fell in a dusty cloud from her talons onto the floor, and several newts grunted and covered their faces in protest. Desperate, Juni shook her head, releasing spittle onto the sand.

"Juni," Rock interrupted. Juni turned to face her. "Waterfall." Rock made the sound of a faucet. No, not a faucet. Like a mountain stream. "A waterfall?"

At Rock's sound Juni hopped and returned to Tum's side. Leader, her hands twitching and face pulled tight, sat back on the stump, barking something at another newt.

This newt stepped over and spoke to Tum. Softly at first and then with increased intensity.

"Yes, that's it. The waterfall tunnel is the safest. It is a long passage, and weak and slow pyrsi will need things. Um, food and water. Supplies, I guess." Tum glanced apologetically at Dime.

"That makes sense," Dime answered, smiling reassuringly at her child. "Tell them we'll get supplies from the fairies, enough for Juni and Stern Eyes also. We won't need anything from the troop."

Leader stood up on the stump and held still, as if waiting for something to happen. Dime glanced over at Stern Eyes, hoping for some guidance. What now? Should they just leave? Should there be words? She'd already given Leader a gift. Had that been too soon? Was another gift requested? This was more stressful than staying at one of those high-class vacation towers.

Stern Eyes raised her arms and howled. Juni joined in, and soon the whole room was howling. Dime was not about to join this; she had no idea what was going on. But when Stern Eyes marched from the shelter, she and the group followed, trudging up the long slope toward the forest until they were out of sight.

"Ma-ma, we're going to get Agni and our bags and come back,"

Tum said. She made no illusion of asking, so Dime nodded as Juni and Tum ran off.

"Newts!" Rock said, under her breath.

Luja laughed. "I know."

Dime wasn't even really used to them, but she could only stay befuddled about so many things at a time. "Ok, yes, newts, but now that we have an idea where to go, do we leave right away?"

"No." Rock sounded softer than normal. "No. We're very tired and we need supplies. Let's get back to Volana's and see if there's somewhere we can stock up." She gazed down the hill, waiting until Juni ran up again, two bags bouncing from her arm, Tum in her grasp, and Agni's furry head peeking out from Tum's cloth sling.

"Tum," Rock asked her, "would Stern Eyes be able to understand meeting us somewhere? I'm concerned what might happen taking them into Pito."

Rock was rubbing her elbows again and appeared distressed. Dime understood that. There were too many tracks of worry, carrying on over too many cycles. They weren't used to this, and she was pretty sure they never should be.

"Yes," Tum said, looking surprised. "Oh, yes, they'll understand. That's the sort of thing they mostly do. I'll ask them where we should meet, and you can tell me if it makes sense to you."

A take or so later, they'd worked out that the newts would rest also, then meet them at a waterfall to the sur side of Pito. Tum seemed to think they were communicating a caution. "They keep saying they'll need to hide, but they'll find us when we arrive. But they seem nervous. Maybe being near the city. Near the fairies, I guess. Since they could be seen."

"We'll work it out," Dime said. "Tell them we'll be there. Between this clever crew, we'll figure a way." She tried to sound enthusiastic. It would also be daylight by then, and she didn't know if that would work for them or against them. She was leaning toward *for,* as the idea of finding a waterfall tunnel in the dark had not sounded appealing.

"Does everyone understand this trip is dangerous?" she added. "We're going to find a weapon. Whatever it is, that puts us all at risk. I also ask for everyone's agreement that when we find the room, only I will go in."

"We trust your judgment, and we will then," Rock said with a hardness to her eyes, "but we're not putting anyone at risk with a set of preconditions. If we're going to go, you have to trust us too."

Responding to Tum, Stern Eyes expressed similar sentiments. At least it sounded that way. Dime relented. But what could she really say? Everyone was at risk. Every one of them. She hoped they'd trust her about the room, though. Rock knew the possibility it held the curse, and she'd told Luja. She refused to tell Tum, as she didn't want her to be scared while they were gone. She'd tell her once they destroyed it. And the newts hadn't pressed for detail; Dime's statement that it was bad seemed enough.

"Well, if we're ready, I have to go that way first." She pointed. "And get our bench. Tum, Luja, Rock, I think we can all fit if we hold our bags on our laps and squeeze in tight. Just wait here and I'll be back. Juni, Stern Eyes, we'll see you soon."

It was still dark as they landed on the walkway that wound around Volana's home, and Dime was surprised to see that her ramp had already been lowered down, creating a path to the ground level. Still, they landed on the walkway above. After pushing the bench back against the outer wall, Dime whispered into the curtain. Without doors, Dime didn't know how you could tell if a fairy was open to visitors. She'd have to ask that. She heard voices inside, so it didn't seem that anyone was asleep. Actually, there were several voices. She wondered if they should leave.

Dime glanced out into the trees and at the ground below, glad to see no signs anyone was watching them or had followed. She'd used the last of her energy concentrating on not being seen. She hoped to Sol they could avoid being seen by someone who could alert Neimano.

Volana emerged onto the walkway, a tired smile on her face. "Come in. Uchitar is still here and my mothers decided to visit." She paused. "I'm sorry. I love for my mothers to visit, but I'm just also very tired." She yawned.

Only then did she seem to notice the waiting crowd. "Tum. Luja. Rock! What a lovely surprise to see everyone. Please, come in."

As the others filed past, Dime took the moment to beckon Volana to the other side of the door. "I'll explain more, but we're going somewhere dangerous and I can't take Tum. Or won't. Either way, she doesn't have her chair. I feel bad imposing, but if there's any way you can get her back to Lodon or—"

"This is perfect." She leaned in.

Dime had no idea what—

"My mothers are in a coddling mood, and I do not even have a baby yet." She pointed down. "Also, they have ramps at their home. If, of course, you would trust your child with them?"

"I have no concern." While Dime would rather get Tum back to Batu's and to her chair, Volana probably had enough going on right now. And with all her isolation that Dime was not yet able to fix, Tum would probably love being coddled by Ga-mas. "Thank you. I'll make this up to you."

Volana waved a hand. "The gift is maybe I can sleep?" She stood straighter. "Unless you need my help?"

"I don't need you to go," Dime said, thinking through how to put this. Given the connection to the Seats, she hadn't yet decided whether Volana should know what they are off to do, or whether that would only put them all at risk. She decided to stay vague until she could think it through more. "Sorry, I don't know how to say all of this, so I'll just be direct. We know of an imminent danger to Pito—to all of us—and we plan to go resolve it. We're in need of supplies, and I'd rather not take the time to return to Sol's Reach right now, let alone Lodon. Can anyone help?"

"Yes," Volana answered, more quickly and confidently than Dime could have expected. She certainly didn't expect Volana to break into a grin. "Yes, I think so. Should we go in?"

Dime nodded and made her way through the curtain. To a very crowded room.

Volana's mothers—assuming that's who the two unknown fairies were—were gasping in surprise and delight at the arrival of the solies. Rock was holding both hands with one of them, telling her about something. Tum was climbing up onto the bench, and Luja was jammed into a corner murmuring to Uchitar, who was scanning the room with a blank expression. Agni, for once, looked overwhelmed, crouched beneath a table, only her ears and the shine from her eyes poking out from the shadow.

Coaxing them away, Volana pulled her mothers into her sleeping area.

"What a night!" Rock smiled.

Yes, what a night indeed. One that had started by untying Rock from Jaza's strange clutches and ended witnessing her being smothered by fairy mothers. In addition, the fact that a great amount of their group smelled like Sha water was more pronounced in the small space, though Dime noted none of the fairies had raised the point. Hopefully Volana's mothers didn't think all solies smelled this way.

She glanced again at Uchitar, but he was still occupied talking to Luja. The three fe'pyrsi returned to the room, and Volana raised her hands. Everyone fell silent.

"This is too many pyrsi and kita for my home," she said. Dime tried to imagine if she'd seen the newts there, too. "Tum, my friend, will you go with my mothers for a while? They said Agni can stay with them too, if she would like."

Tum glanced over at Dime in a mix of dismay and delight, as if she'd been expecting Dime not to take her, but had quickly decided living in a fairy tree home for a while might be an acceptable trade. "Yes that would be nice," she said to Volana. Maybe Luja wasn't the only one growing up.

As everyone resumed talking, Dime pulled Tum aside.

"Hey. Don't be mad at me. I'm already going to worry about Luja the whole time; can you help me not worry about you?"

"I know," Tum said. "I'm not mad."

Grateful, Dime reached down and squeezed her child in a deep hug.

"Everyone else," Volana continued, "I am about to take up an offer. Do what you need for now, then we will leave."

With many hugs from the whole group, Tum and Agni waited with Volana's mothers to be picked up by a group of fliers, who seemed, from what Dime could hear, to assume Tum's lack of wings related to her not having legs, with no understanding she was a soly.

They pulled the ramp back up and straightened up the small room, before all moving out to the walkway. "You're sure you don't need me to go with you?" Volana asked.

"I'm sure," Dime said. "You're needed here."

"May I go?" Uchitar's voice trembled. "Please. I'd like to go. I'd like to help."

Volana looked as though she were going to answer, but she stopped. In her eyes, Dime read conflict. It had been less than a turn, though that felt hard to believe, since they'd taken the pyr, nearly unconscious, from the Seats' prison. No, he still didn't look well.

Yet there were no Fo-ror currently in the group going. It was hard to say how that knowledge might help, given their proximity to the complex. But would Uchitar be well enough? He appeared worn and shaky but he was back on his feet.

Volana looked so tired.

"It's going to be dangerous," Dime said. "Going could risk . . . our lives." Saying that knowing her child would accompany them pained her more than she could express. Yet, all lives were precious. Rock's. Stern Eyes'. Juni's. Her own.

"I'd like to go," was all the fairy said, his eyes darting around.

Volana was giving him a long stare. A whole silent conversation passed between them, and the fe'pyr finally turned around, as if relenting.

"I'll go if you'll have me," he repeated.

Dime nodded and Uchitar's arms fell to his sides. "Where to, Volana?" she asked.

"Someone recently asked us what we needed. Anything he could do, he said. We will go now and call in that favor."

Dime wondered who this pyr could be. But she didn't want to press. "Do you think he's ready for us?"

Volana did not smile. "No." And with a flap of her wings, she left the walkway and rose into the night.

END OF PART 08

ABOUT THE AUTHOR

E.D.E. Bell (she/e) was born in the year of the fire dragon during a Cleveland blizzard. After a youth in the mitten, an MSE in Electrical Engineering from the University of Michigan, three wonderful children, and nearly two decades in Northern Virginia and Southwest Ohio developing technical intelligence strategy, she now applies her magic to the creation of genre-bending fantasy fiction in Ferndale, Michigan, where she is proud to be part of the Detroit arts community. A passionate vegan and enthusiastic denier of gender rules, she feels strongly about issues related to human equality and animal compassion. She revels in garlic. She loves cats and trees. You can follow her adventures at edebell.com.

Continue Dime's story in . . .

Part 09: Depths

edebell.com/diamondsong